Black Wolf Moon

Duke Charles

Black Wolf Moon

For information about this title or to order other books
and/or electronic media, contact the publisher:

Twin Eagle Promotions
New Braunfels, TX 78130
www.DukeCharles.com
DukeCharlesWriter@gmail.com

ISBNs
Softcover: 978-1-947201-24-8
eBook:978-1-947201-25-5

Printed in the United States of America

To all my kids, Lisa, Brad, and Brett, thank you so very, very much for not ever asking for money.

I love y'all!

Truly, Dad

Prologue

The giant black wolf moved stealthily over the boulders and through the heavy brush. The moon's reflection shined bright red in his eyes. Terry lay unconscious wedged between two large rocks; the bullet hole in her left shoulder had been shot clean and clear through, and the blood ran crimson red in the light from the dark Montana moon. The smell of the fresh blood oozing from Teresa's wound was strong in the wolf's nose, which led the big animal on toward her location, but it had something else to tend to first.

The three poachers had taken cover a couple hundred yards further up the mountain; they were dragging five black wolf pelts with them as they went that were each worth over $500 on the black market, which meant they would profit much from their kills.

Mashti, which means "sweet person" in Cherokee, stood on a large rock 15 feet above the wolf killers, looking down on them ready to pounce. He was aware that Terry needed his assistance, but he felt like this situation required his full attention and should be handled first.

The men huddled together, focused all their attention down the mountain and had no idea that 125 pounds of solid muscle was hurtling through the air about to attack them with all its fury!

Chapter 1

Teresa Littrel was 5'4" and a 120 pounds of solid muscle with a figure that could have been formed by one of the Greek master sculptors. She was born in 1986 in Milo, Missouri, which was a small town of around 1500 friendly folks. The fact that she was almost full-blooded Cherokee Indian except for a great grandmother from Scotland many moons ago as well as the fact that she was absolutely gorgeous, just made her that much more interesting. Her ancestors were forced to march down the Trail Of Tears in 1837-38, and the survivors settled in and around Cape Girardeau, Missouri.

She really thought she would die in this part of the country, riding her horses and raising her African pygmy goats for show, selling the two quarts of extremely rich butterfat milk (almost 6 %) that each of her seven does produced every day. She had people waiting in line for fresh goat milk most days, and she priced it based on the way she felt when she stepped out of bed each morning. She would be turning 31 in a week or so, which means this story begins in the spring of 2017.

After 12 years of starting and then dropping out of classes at a state college, she finally received a bachelor's degree in law enforcement and criminal investigation. Now the decision was what to do with all her new-found knowledge. She actually was pretty happy on her grandpa's farm with little or no responsibility although a little more income for maintenance would be better.

It was just her, 10 small goats, and her two horses that lived on the farm. One of her horses was a very large gold and white paint mountain horse that reminded her of biscuits and gravy, so she called him Biscuit. The other one was a very smart, off-white pack horse she called Gravy because she thought it was funny, and it made her smile every time she thought of them together.

She had sent off some resumés over the last year but didn't really expect to hear from any of the major police departments, and she really didn't want to move to a big city anyway.

Shortly after graduation on a sunny day, she and Biscuit were riding close to the road that passed the farm when Molly, the postal gal, flagged her down and handed her a half a dozen envelopes, and Terry, as she preferred to be called, stuffed them inside her George Strait western shirt and touched Biscuit on the flanks, and they headed for the barn about a quarter of a mile away. The large horse put his head down and found a gate that Terry seldom let him enter, mainly because it was so fast, that it almost scared her when she rode him bareback. Almost.

She was sitting on her bed in her room on the second floor of her grandpa's run-down farmhouse, and she began to sort her mail: three rejections, a credit card statement for $68, most of which was for pizza from Pizza Hut, and one possibility if she would check back with that department in six months. She almost overlooked the very official looking manila envelope that had managed to slip three-quarters of the way under her pillow. She opened the envelope and pulled out the very official-looking letter addressed to her:

Montana Department of Justice,
Attorney General, Gerald R. Abbott
PO Box 241
Helena, Montana 59601

Miss Teresa Littrel
RR 14
Milo Missouri, 64767

The message that was very short and to the point read:

Miss T. Littrel,
We would like to offer you a position with the Montana Department of Justice. This position is working with and controlling the treatment of animals and livestock in the state of Montana.
If this sounds like something you might be interested in, please contact me before April 15th, 2017.
With regards,
Gerald R. Abbott,
Attorney General for the State of Montana

The letter also contained what looked to be a cell phone number because she didn't recognize the area code. She checked the date on her phone. She had almost lost track of the days as there really wasn't much use for the date out on the farm. The date was the 10th of April. She wondered where the time had gone.

She let the job offer run around her brain for a second:

"Riding around Montana, making sure no one abused any cows, chickens, or goats? How bad could that be? I wish my gramps was here to talk this over with," she thought almost out loud.

Gramps had a way of finding the answers to a lot of questions as she thought he had some special connection with the Great Spirit and always seemed to come up with a special answer that she would not have thought of in a thousand years.

"So what do ya think, Gramps?" and she smiled, knowing he couldn't answer her. Then the lamp on the small table beside her bed went out; what a time for a bulb to go bad! Terry reached over and tapped it with the palm of her hand and nothing. Then out of habit, she push the switch under the shade, and it came back on and startled the hell out of her. WHAT? She flipped the switch on and off several times, and each time it worked as if it were a brand-spanking new bulb, "Grandpa? Is that you? Don't mess with me!"

She took her cue from the "flickering light bulb" "This is Jerry Abbott; how may I help you?"

"Mr. Abbott, this is Terry Littrel in Milo, Missouri. I received a letter from you today regarding a job opportunity. Is that position still available?"

"Why, yes, Miss Littrell, it is."

"Oh, please, sir, call me Terry."

"Well, Terry, how would you feel about traveling around Montana in a pickup truck with a trailer for a home and working for me?"

"Well, sir, I don't know you, but I do love being outdoors and on my own and having a nice warm home with me sounds very interesting."

"Wonderful! There is a four-week class on Federal Law and Training in Washington D.C. that starts two weeks from today. The week after you complete that class, you will need to take a two-week class up here in Montana. Do you suppose you could get your affairs in order by then?"

"Yes, sir! I'm sure I could if all the benefits are satisfactory."

They talked for over an hour and then Mr. Jerry Abbott said, "Let me email you a list of the benefits and a contract for you to look over, and we'll talk again tomorrow. How does that sound, Miss...ah...I mean...Terry?"

"Yes, sir, that would be fine. I'll look for your email..." and before she finished her sentence, her computer beeped notifying her she received a new email.

"Ah, was that you, sir?"

"I believe it was; look it over, and I'll call you at 10 tomorrow morning. Will that work?"

"Yes, sir. That'll work just fine," and the line went dead.

All this was coming at her so fast! She shook her head and headed for the fridge to get a beer. She sat at the small desk and fired up her laptop, and there it was: the email from *grabbott@montana.gov*.

The first things she noticed in the email were the attachments. The first few were several photographs of a brand-new, Ford F-350 King Ranch, super-crew cab with a long bed and dual wheels that was setup for hauling. The second attachment was a picture of a fifth wheel, two horse trailer with living quarters that looked brand-spanking new as well, "Holy crap! These guys don't mess around! I guess I better consider giving them 100 percent," she thought to herself as her head spun, trying to figure what to do with the farm and her goats because her horses were coming with her, period!

Chapter 2

The next morning, Teresa Littrel received the phone call from Jerry Abbott right on time.

"Good morning, Terry!"

She looked at her watch, "9:59 and 40 seconds, amazing!" she thought.

"Well, young lady, what do you think?"

"I THINK you made a mistake; this contract says I'm on half pay until I finish training, and then my salary is $76,000 a year to start. Is that right?"

"Yes, but only for the first year, and if that's not satisfactory, I could probably get you a little more."

"How much more?" Terry asked just out of curiosity.

"How about another 20k?" Abbott asked, and Terry almost choked on the fresh cup of coffee she had just taken a sip of.

"But you have to remember that all your expenses are picked up by the state, every single one."

"So, you're telling me that you are gonna put $96,000 in my bank account each year, and all I have to do is ride around the beautiful state of Montana and make sure people aren't having sexual relations with their sheep or abusing their dogs?"

"That's pretty much it, except of course, for the poachers and rustlers and the dog and chicken fighters and the trappers who are trying to wipe out the wolf and bear population."

"Well...ok. I guess there are still some things I have to learn about the government and fighting crime and arresting poachers."

They talked for over two hours, and Terry explained about her connection with her goats and Biscuit and Gravy (her horses) and that she wasn't sure what to do with the farm, but she had some ideas.

When they hung up, she printed out the documents in duplicate and put one copy in her desk drawer, took the other one, and headed to town to meet with Randy Lesh, a 50-something year old attorney who specialized in land and inheritance cases. However, in a rural area that small, he basically handled just about anything except murder cases.

When she walked into Randy's office a half-hour later, he was sitting at his desk. He got up and went over to shake her hand:

"Teresa, how are you my dear? I haven't seen you in years, not since yer gramps passed except to wave at you on the highway," he said with a warm smile.

"Yes, Mr. Lesh, I'm fine. It is good to see you as well."

"Please, call me Randy; how can I be of service today?"

"I received a job offer from the state of Montana, and I was hoping you could look over the contract to make sure I'm not overlooking anything. I'd normally rely on Gramps for this sort of thing, but of course, he's out of touch," then she remembered the desk lamp and smiled to herself.

"Absolutely! I'd be happy to! Have a seat, and we'll have a look."

The four-page document was very straightforward, and after every paragraph, Randy would pause and scratch his balding crew cut and make a gurgling noise in his throat, then mutter, "Uh-huh, uh-huh."

"Would you like me to come back later?"

"Oh no! I'll be finished in a couple of minutes. You know, it looks to me like you stepped in a pile of cow plop and are coming out smelling like a bouquet of valley flowers! I mean they're offering insurance, a 401K retirement package, plus yer expenses, and $96,000 a year to boot from the state of Montana? Sweetheart deals like this don't come along every day, and unless you have a problem relocating, I'd say jump on it!"

"Thank you so much, Randy! How much do I owe you?"

"Just go give 'em hell, girl! That'll be plenty enough for me! Oh, and by the way...what are yer plans for yer grandaddy's, I mean yer farm?"

"I'm not sure just yet; I don't really want to sell it because I may want to come back to it someday."

"I have an idea: there's this nice young couple in town who just had a new baby, and he's losing his job because the big Walmart store is forcing McGuire's Hardware to close their doors, and the couple is being evicted from their rent house as well. I can give you their address if you like. Maybe they could move into your farm house and take care of things while you are gone."

"That would be great, Randy!"

He checked his computer screen and scribbled down the couple's names and address on a piece of scratch paper and handed it to Terry, "Tell them I said 'howdy' and to call me if I can do anything, will ya?"

"I sure will, Randy, and thanks again for everything!"

"Don't mention it and go up to the mountains and make us proud!"

"I'll do my best!"

Terry stepped up into her 2001 Ford F-150 and took her seat then looked at the note from Randy the attorney.

"Larry & Kathy Douglass...303 King St. That's only about six block from here," she turned the key in the ignition, and the engine fired right up. With a 160K on the odometer, it amazed her how reliable her old truck had been and still was.

Three minutes later, she sat in front of a very small, well-kept clapboard house; the yard was maintained down to the sidewalks that were trimmed to a tee. The rose bushes were in bloom, and she could tell that someone had put a lot of time and effort into keeping the place up. "Pride," she thought, "Nothing like it."

She walked up on the wooden stoop and knocked on the door. Right away, a very attractive young girl in her early twenties with a new baby in her arms answered the door, and her smile beamed.

"Hi there! How can I help you today?"

Teresa thought, "Wow! If they're broke and about to lose everything, you'd never know it!" It certainly didn't show on this pretty young thing's face.

"Hi there. I'm Terry Littrel, and Randy Lesh, the city attorney, gave me your address and thought we may be able to help each other out."

"Please come in, Miss Littrel; can I get you a glass of sweet tea?"

"If you'll join me, I'd be pleased to have a glass with you."

She disappeared into the kitchen, and Terry took a look around the squeaky-clean, combination living and dining room and then took a seat at a nice quality but well-worn dining room table that only needed a little refinishing, and it would be as good as new. Terry had an eye for good furniture as her gramps was a master at building, repairing, and refinishing fine furniture. He made the majority of his income from working with wood, and his shop was still 100% in tact out on the farm.

Just then she heard the screen door open and another voice in the kitchen. A short, stocky man not much taller than herself came out with a big smile on his sunburned face. He reminded her of a fireplug, and he looked as solid as one.

"Miss Littrel, I'm Larry Douglass, but you can call me Tank."

"I wonder why?" she asked, and they both laughed out loud. She responded with,"Please call me Terry."

A few seconds later, Kathy came out from the kitchen with a tray of iced tea in one hand and their beautiful little girl in the other.

"Forgive my coveralls. I've been over at the neighbors cuttin grass; they're just too old to take care of their yard any longer, so I try to help out, and I kinda take a likin to outdoor work," Tank said.

"Tank, let me get right to the point," she took a sip of the best sweet tea she could remember ever tasting that had just a hint of mint and a taste of lemon and very special. "I'm about to accept a job in Montana and will have to relocate, and I'm looking for someone to take care of my farm. I don't want to sell it as I may decide to come back to it someday."

The couple looked at each other, and tears came to Kathy's eyes.

Tank spoke up, "I have always wanted to live and work on a farm but never had the opportunity, but I'm afraid we wouldn't be able to pay you rent. You see, I just lost my very low-paying job down at the hardware store, and we have been asked to leave this place by the end of the week. I'm so sorry."

"Don't be sorry, Tank, just hear me out...I have a three-bedroom farm house that sits on about 50 acres with some corn and a pretty nice garden and 10 pigmy goats that need to be looked after, and all I would ask is that you take care of the place."

"How much would you be asking in rent? Maybe we could borrow enough to get moved in and settled?"

"I don't think you understand. I don't want to rent it to you. I want to give it to you to be the caretakers and live there."

"You want to give us a place to live? A farm?" and the tears truly began to stream down Kathy's face.

"Yes, that is right! Would you like to go take a look before you make a decision?"

"We would love to see it, but our old car is on its last leg and out of gas, and Tank has been walking to work and back for the last three months, trying to save enough to get it tuned up."

"That's not a problem. Why don't you gather up some diapers for the baby and whatever else you need and let's take a ride out to the farm. By the way, there's plenty of goat milk out there too."

Terry got them all loaded up in her truck and took off down the road. Kathy looked around, "This is a really nice truck," she commented.

"Thanks. It was my grandpa's; he passed away about three years ago, and oh, by the way...it goes with the farm, so yer transportation problems should be taken care of as well."

Oh Lord! More tears!

"Kathy...where is all that water coming from?"

"I'm sorry, Terry, but you took us completely by surprise. We were at the end of our rope without enough money to move to a new place, even if we could find one, which we couldn't."

"Well, don't worry! I have a feeling this is going to work out for all of us!"

Tank sat in the passenger's seat with his hands over his eyes. Terry wasn't sure if he was praying or crying, and then the tears started leaking between his fingers, and she decided that maybe it was a little of both. "Dang...this is the cryinest family I've ever seen!"

Kathy and the precious baby girl sat in the back seat of the old pickup with like-new interior. Her grandpa kept it very clean, and Terry did the same to honor him.

"Oh my God!" Kathy gasped as Terry turned down the drive, "We have been by this farm a hundred times and have always admired it! It is just the perfect size for a family our size to take care of!" and there came the waterworks again.

They inspected the barn and stable and then the two-story farmhouse.

"Do you suppose you could get by with just the bottom floor? It's about 1800 square feet with three bedrooms. I'd kinda like to keep the upstairs for my things until I know how the new job goes."

"Are you serious?" Kathy came back. "It's a mansion compared to what we are used to, and Tank is an incredible handyman; he can fix anything!"

"I noticed that some of the furniture in your house could stand some sanding and staining; do you work with wood?"

"Oh, that's not our furniture; it belongs to the landlord, but Tank is a furniture maker, and he does repairs too."

"Well then, follow me," and Terry led them out the back door to a large metal building that the young couple had not noticed. Inside, Terry flipped the switch on the wall, and several overhead neon lights lit up a 45 x 30 shop equipped with the best of saws, sanders, paint sprayers, and hand tools of every sort to do professional woodworking. Tank's face lit up and of course, Kathy started to cry, again!

"Oh, and there's a list of Gramp's most recent customers over on the desk; you might call and scare up some business, if you are so inclined."

Terry pulled open the door on a very large side-by side-commercial freezer to reveal a dozen pizzas stacked on one side, individual freezer packs of steaks, hamburger meat, pork chops, assorted vegetables and fruits, and everything a country family would need to eat healthy for months.

"Hope ya'll are hungry!" and the tears started to flow once again.

Two weeks later, Tank drove Terry the 50 miles to the Joplin International Airport where a private jet was waiting to shuttle her to Quantico, Virginia, to the FBI Academy to begin her training.

Chapter 3

At the FBI Academy at Quantico, Terry endured four weeks of pushups, sit-ups, and running five miles twice a day plus the four hours of classroom studies learning state and federal law. As it turned out, Terry was training to become a full-fledged, United States federal agent and investigator if she didn't perish somewhere along the way. Moreover, she was probably in the best shape of any recruit to ever come through the academy, and she finished first in her class of fifteen.

Four weeks later, she put a black, plastic, trash bag full of her khaki shorts and pants and six navy polo shirts with *Recruit* screen-printed in gold over the pocket and a couple pair of black sneakers into a trash can at the exit from the ladies' room. As quickly as she could, she changed into her Wranglers and a comfortable white western shirt and her brown, leather, Tony Lama boots, and thought to herself, "Please, God, don't ever make me have to wear khaki again!"

The private jet was in the same exact spot at the airport where it let Terry off four weeks earlier. This time, there was a noticeable difference in her demeanor. Her raven-black hair was shorter, not even touching her shoulders; her waist seemed smaller, and her shoulders seemed broader, and she walked with an air of confidence that she hadn't had in the past. There was a gold and silver badge clipped to her wide western belt that read *U.S. Federal Agent,* and a Glock 26, .9mm with two magazines in a special paddle holster on her right hip.

Most of the other recruits opted for a Glock 19 that held 15 rounds, but Terry was a small girl, and the 26 with only 10-round mags seemed like the best fit to her. Besides, if the situation was so heated that nine rounds wouldn't solve the problem, she decided she'd put the tenth one in her ear anyway.

Tank and Kathy and that beautiful little girl were waiting for her just outside the gate of the private entrance when she arrived back home. Grandpa's truck looked like new as it had been washed and waxed, and Terry really wasn't surprised; she wouldn't have expected any less from the Douglass's.

The 45-minute ride back to Milo was filled with excited tales of how wonderful farm life was and how kind the country folk had been to the couple, and of course, there were tears, always more tears!

"Kathy, what the hell are you crying about now?" Terry asked.

"Terry, I'm just so happy! We'll never be able to repay you for all you've done for us."

"Well, unless the place has burned down in the last four weeks, I'd say we're even!"

When they turned into the drive, Terry immediately spotted the changes. The barn, stable, and farmhouse had a new coat of paint, and things just looked better all around. The grass in the pastures was shorter, and all the shrubs and flowers around the property were trimmed and blossoming, and everything looked like new. Terry counted the goats in the outside pen, and it turned out that there were more than when she left.

"What happened?"

Tank spoke up, "One of yer grandad's customers wanted to trade out some baby goats for having her dining room set refinished, and I couldn't think of any reason why not to trade; hope you don't mind?"

"Mind? Why hell, Tank! It looks like we're in the goat business, partner!"

Tank smiled and said, "Yes ma'am!" and of course, Kathy cried. Sweet Jesus!

As Terry expected, the inside of the house was spotless as well.

"We haven't had a chance to finish all the rooms downstairs. We still have the kitchen and the guest bedroom to go, but it'll be done soon; we did get the upstairs all done, so I hope you'll be comfortable up there."

"You people are crazy! Do you work all night or what?" Nothing but smiles from the Douglass's and of course, more tears.

Terry spent the best part of the next week riding Biscuit with Gravy close behind; they even spent a night camped on the river, and she was completely relaxed; in fact, she was so at home, she began to wonder if she had made a mistake in taking the job. Oh well, it was too late now.

The flight from Joplin to Helena would take five hours and 45 minutes by commercial carrier, but the Lear made it in just over four hours, which was a pretty enjoyable way to travel. Terry thought she could get used to that if worse came to worse. Maybe they had decided to give her an airplane instead of a pickup and trailer? Not!

A really big, black, GMC, SUV with blacked out windows and four rows of seats was waiting for her outside the gate at the private hangar in Helena, Montana. A 6'4" cowboy in jeans and boots was standing there with the door behind the passenger seat open, "Miss Littrel? I'm jasper Green. Mr. Abbott asked me to deliver you to him."

"Howdy, Jasper!" and she stuck out her hand and they shook. Jasper's grip was strong, but not as strong as she expected. Maybe he was just holding back? She would see.

She looked in the open door, "Just the two of us, Jasper?"

"Yes, ma'am! Just us chickens."

"Well then, I believe I'll ride up front like a grown up," and she pushed the door shut and moved to the front. Jasper stood looking half surprised and half impressed, "I believe I'm gonna like this one!" he thought to himself.

"Terry! So glad to meet you!" a 60-something man in a grey, tweed, sport coat with leather patches on the elbow's and a shooter's patch on the right shoulder stood waiting for her with a huge smile. He was wearing jeans and very expensive western boots. He stood in front of her, and he was maybe 6'2," and she could tell he had once been a very strong hombre in his youth. Hell, maybe he still was. Anyway, she liked him from the get-go.

"I guess you met Jasper, did ya? He's gonna be yer guide for the next couple a weeks or so. By the way, congratulations on acing that little party over in Virginia. I had a feeling you would."

"Thank you, sir. It kind of caught me by surprise. I thought I was in pretty good shape, but those folks get down right serious over there."

"Well you look like you came through it with flying colors, my dear. Teresa Littrel, Federal Agent and Investigator, welcome aboard!"

"Thank you sir, but I was under the impression that I would be working for the state of Montana."

"Oh, you will be for as long as we need you, or until you want out, but you are a federal employee, if that's ok with you?"

"I guess it's kinda late to worry about that now, already done the hard stuff."

"Yep, that's right!" and Jerry gave her an almost sinister grin, and all of a sudden, Terry wasn't quite as sure about liking this guy after all. "You'll be working directly FOR me and reporting only TO me; is that clear?"

"Yes, sir."

"There are some folks in this part of the country who are not too concerned about how they make their money, and the less they know about our little operation the better. Please, Terry, have a seat," and as she made it to the nearest chair, Jerry pulled an almost full bottle of Crown Royal Reserve from his desk drawer along with two glasses and poured a very generous amount of the amber liquid in each of their glasses. "What's yer poison of choice, gal?"

"Well, sir, right now, I'd have to say it's Crown," and Jerry Abbott smiled. He knew he'd made the right choice in choosing Miss Teresa Littrel.

Jerry Abbott pushed a button on his desk, and three seconds later, Jasper came walking through the door and took a seat next to Terry. Abbott retrieved another glass from his desk drawer, poured the same amount of Crown into it, and slid the glass in Jasper's direction, "Jasper, here, is going to show you the ropes over the next two weeks or so, and you can trust him, if you know what I mean."

"Yes, sir! I believe I do!"

The three toasted and downed the warm-tasting liquid, and Terry wondered why she had never done the Crown Royal thing. Maybe it was the price, "Don't believe that will be an issue anymore," and she smiled and felt warm inside.

"We reserved a room for you at the Hilton, and if you're up to it, I'll pick you up for dinner after a while."

Terry turned to look at Jasper, "Well, Mr. Green, don't you have a family to get home to?"

"Nope! It's just me and a couple of ol' nags over in the stalls."

She turned back to Abbott, "Well sir, I truly am hearing some moans from my belly; it's been awhile since my last meal, so if you are inclined to wait when you haul me to my hotel room, I'll clean up really quick and put on a clean shirt, and we can go eat now."

She looked at her watch and saw that it was going on 6 o'clock; no wonder she was hungry. That bowl of oatmeal, orange juice, and two cups of joe that Kathy fixed her at six that morning was used up hours ago.

"Probably the best steaks in the state are right up the street at Grizzlies, if that's ok with you?" Jasper commented.

"Jasper, if you put a steak in front of me, you better not leave yer hand holding the plate for too long, if ya get my drift?"

"Sure do, Miss Terry!" and they were off.

Jasper was 100% correct: a two-pound porterhouse and the biggest Idaho potato Terry had ever seen came out on a sizzling, cast-iron skillet about 14 inches across with a big chunk of fresh butter melting on top of the perfectly charred slab of prime beef. Terry wasn't sure if she was hallucinating or whether she had died and gone to heaven, but she had never seen a steak that big before then.

"Think you can handle that?" Jasper asked with a wry grin on his face. "Ya know, sometimes we have to go for a week or two without eating, so ya better get used to chowin down!"

"A week or two? I don't know about you, but they promised me a trailer, and I'm a pretty fair country cook and not a bad shot either, and I have a certificate from the FBI to prove it! No doubt I'll find something to eat."

They both smiled, and Terry could tell she was beginning to warm to this tall cowboy.

The next morning at 6:30, Terry walked out of the lobby carrying two large cups of joe with her bag slung over her shoulder and found Jasper in his pickup with a large trailer behind not unlike the one that would be waiting for her when she returned home.

"Damn, cowboy! I thought for sure I'd beat you up!" She got in and saw he had also purchased coffee for the both of them.

"Hope ya take yer coffee black," he said.

"Yep! Is there any other way?"

"Sure makes shopping easier!"

"Yeah, it sure does! With all this joe, hope there's a place to pee where we're headed?" she looked hopefully over at him.

"Well, gal, I thought you liked it natural, but there's always the trailer."

"Oh, yeah! I may have to get used to living out of one of those things."

"Have you ever been inside of 'one of those things?'"

"No, can't say I have."

"You're in for a shock! Everything you could ever need is fitted inside that little tin box, and it'll take care of ya in the worst weather as well."

So, with their four cups of coffee, two in the cup holders, and one in each hand, Jasper started the big truck and pulled the shift lever down into *D*, and the diesel powered up, and they were off.

They turned on to US-12 out of Helena, headed west to I-90, and then into Missoula, approximately 95 miles away."

"My God, Jasper! This is the most beautiful country I've ever seen!"

"Yeah? Well, get yer eyes full, because come winter, it won't be nothin but white!"

They rode and talked, and the miles flew by. As it turned out, Jasper was a pretty straight-shooter, and Terry began to feel very fond of him.

"I thought Missouri had a lot of water, but this is crazy; there are rivers everywhere!"

"And lakes, too. Do you fish?"

"Well, I'm pretty good with a cane pole and some stink bait. I have pulled in some pretty big cats out of the river back home."

"What's the biggest you've caught?"

"I have pulled in a couple that were right at 12 pounds."

"Not bad, but baby trout up here weigh about 12 pounds," and Jasper smiled that funny smile that Terry was getting very used to.

"Jasper, are you sure we're not in Texas because yer BS is truly startin to sound like a load of Texas crap!" they both laughed out loud again.

"You gettin hungry, girl?"

"Damn, I thought we might be on that one-week stretch without food you were so proud of. Yeah, I could eat, if you can find something to cook!"

"Best spot in Montana for breakfast is just up at the top of this hill."

"Let's do it! We probably need to check yer horses anyway; don't cha think?"

"They have plenty of feed, but we should check the water tank; sometimes the valve will stick and drain it dry."

At the diner, Terry ordered a four-egg omelet with chorizo and cheese that came with a ton of oven-roasted Idaho taters with onions and bell peppers, and a bowl of country gravy, and all the toast, biscuits, or tortillas she could eat and coffee or tea for just $8. She ate like she really was coming off a one-week fast.

"Ok, I think I can go for another week now!"

"Damn, ladybug! You sure can pack them groceries away!"

"Well, ya know with farm life, sometimes it's a while between meals."

"You may as well get used to it; most of the time out here by yerself, there's not much else to do but eat and drink, of course."

The last half of the trip was all uphill, and although the big diesel made easy work of it, Jasper kept its speed around 55 mph, so he could point out landmarks and points of interest, and Terry entered them on her iPad. He also pointed out places that known criminals hung out and congregate although most of their cases came from reports and complaints by private citizens.

Jasper pulled his rig onto a decent dirt road just a few miles east of Missoula. The big hand-carved sign made of three 2x12s read *T-REX RANCH* with a brand on the right-side, *T/X*.

"This place is owned by the state; we took it over when the owners got too old to run it and moved into town. Anytime yer in the area, you can pull in here and park yer rig and resupply. There is always hot coffee and hot chow and a good supply of ammo and just about anything else you need. They also have a vet on staff and a place to house all kinds of animals while they recuperate, and they will also take care of yer horses. Anything you need, these good folks can provide. We have four other places like this around the state; sometimes you just need a place to hole up because of the weather, so be sure and mark this location on your fancy tablet."

Jasper pulled the rig into one of the three spots that had a 12x15-foot slab and heavy metal roof to pull under with water and electricity hookups.

"They also have some bunks inside and some stalls in the stable for yer animals," Jasper pointed towards a well-kept metal building about 30 yards behind the main ranch house. "Let's go in and say howdy!"

"Hey, Martha! This is Terry Littrel, the new outrider; she'll be on the job in about three weeks."

A middle-aged lady who looked to be in her 50s with short, greying hair and about 30 pounds overweight, probably from eating her own cooking from the smell of things, came up to Terry, grabbed hold of her, and gave her a big ol' grandma hug, which made Terry feel warm and at home at once.

"Aren't you just the prettiest little thing! Welcome to the ranch, sugar!"

"Thank you, ma'am. Nice to meet you."

"Ah damn, girl! Just call me Momma M or Martha; everyone does!"

"Yes, ma'am...I mean...Martha! What is that marvelous smell?" Terry asked.

"Oh, that? I just took an ol' blueberry cobbler out of the oven; come on in the kitchen; Ray's on his way in from the stable, and we'll have some coffee when he gets in."

Ray, or "Pa" as most everyone called him, was the other half of the caretaking team, and he was a flat-out cowboy wearing dirty, mud-encrusted boots, Wrangler jeans, and a jacket with wool lining, and a sweat-soaked, western hat cranked down so far on his head, that his ears were folded over.

"Pa!" Martha said, "This is Terry Littrel, the new outrider."

Ray took off his hat, dropped it on the spotless, wooden, kitchen floor, walked up to Terry, and picked her up off her feet, and said in a manly voice, "Well look at you, girl! If I was 30 years younger, I'd be all over you like flies on honey!"

"If you were 30 years younger, I'd probably letcha!" she said, and everyone laughed.

Martha put out bowls of cobbler with heavy cream and steaming mugs of joe, and although Jasper and Terry weren't hungry, they couldn't help themselves. It was the absolute best cobbler and coffee that she had ever had, bar none!

"Storm's a-comin," Pa said, "Bout three hours out. It's got the look of bein a mean one! Looks like you two got here just in time...gonna come down from the mountains to the east...gonna get cold, too!"

"Think we'll give the horses a little exercise before we put them away," Jasper said, and he and Terry left the ranch house.

The temperature had dropped about 10 or 15 degrees since they arrived at the ranch, and black clouds were forming out over the mountains.

"You'll learn pretty quick to have everything you need with you up here in the big sky country as the weather can change in a heartbeat."

They unloaded Jasper's horses and saddled them as the cold was beginning to get to Terry. She was kicking herself for not being better prepared. Momma M walked up behind her and handed her a western-style wool coat with lambswool lining with a high collar and a pair of doe skin gloves.

"This ol' thing's been lying round here for a spell. I was about to throw it out, but it looks like it should fit you just fine," and she flashed Terry that warm smile and gave her a wink. "Pa said to be careful; don't cut 'er too close."

Terry's eyes were watering, and her nose was running from the frigid wind, and the coat and gloves were a lifesaver. "All I can say is 'thank you,' Martha. I won't be caught off guard again."

"No problem, child."

Jasper's horses were well-trained and tired of being cooped up, so after they had walked them for a hundred yards or so to get the kinks out, Jasper asked, "You ready?"

"Any time you are, cowboy!"

Jasper put his heels to his mount; he didn't need spurs; he cranked his hat down over his ears, and he was off.

Terry held back the good-sized black she was on to get a look at Jasper's horsemanship. He looked like he had been born in the saddle.

"Well...guess we better go, don't cha think?" and the black snorted. She touched its flanks, and they were off headed across the meadow in hot pursuit.

She leaned forward and put her head down over her mount's shoulders to break the wind. Jasper eased up on his horse to look over his left shoulder to see what had happened to his companion just as Terry blew by him on his right. He nudged the big strawberry roan and asked, "You gettin old, or what, letting her get by ya?" and he yelled, "Yeeehaa!" and they were off!

What a great feeling it was to have a good horse under her with lots of open land to run on. It was almost like Terry and her new friend were on the same wavelength, and she could tell the horses felt the same.

Jasper's mount was just naturally faster than the black, but Terry gave him a good run for his money until they caught her about a mile or so down the line. They pulled up just as the first big lightning flash hit, and Jasper counted the seconds till he heard the thunder, "Twelve miles away. We need to head fer the barn; it's gonna be close!" he yelled.

"Lead the way; we'll be right beside ya!"

About 50 yards from the stable, the rain began to hit Terry in the face, and they made it inside as the bottom fell out of the bucket, and rain started coming down in sheets.

"You sit a purdy good saddle there, ladybug."

"Yeah, well, yer not so bad yerself, cowboy! I could really get used to this life."

They hung the tac over a sawhorse, combed and brushed the horses, and made sure they had plenty of feed and water then waited for a break in the rain to make a run for the house.

"Girl, you need a hat!" and Martha led her to a small bedroom that was filled with jackets, hats, gloves and shelves full of ammo for pistols, rifles, and shotguns and a rack of weapons in one corner of the room.

"Where did all this stuff come from?"

"Most of it was confiscated from the bad guys, and the rest, the state sends us on a regular basis; help yerself to anything you need; that's what it's here for."

"Thank you, Martha."

"Please, child, call me Momma."

Terry smiled, "Yes, Momma."

Martha came to her and gave her a big hug that lasted a little longer than normal, and Terry saw a tear in her eye when she backed away.

"Are you ok, Momma?"

"Yes, child, I'm fine; you just remind me of someone, that's all."

Terry found a brown Stetson 4x beaver with an extra wide brim that had a "Gus" crease that fit her just perfectly. She looked over the supplies in the store room and then walked out to the kitchen to join the others.

Pa piped up, "Damn! Now, that's one fine-lookin cowgirl right there!"

Terry blushed and bowed.

And Jasper chimed in, "Yeah, and she's the real deal, too! Sits a horse as good as anybody I've ever seen!"

That night, the wind howled, and the rain came in sideways. The temperature settled around freezing, but the wind chill made it feel like zero and at sunup, it wasn't any warmer.

Terry awoke in a strange bed in a strange room, and it took a second to clear the cobwebs and focus. She dressed and headed for the kitchen, and she could smell the coffee and biscuits cooking and had a hunch there was country sausage gravy to go with them, "Don't get no better than that!" she thought.

"Is it as nasty out as it sounds?" she asked as Ray came busting through the back door.

"Damn! That's some kind of weather! Got yer horses and the other stock taken care of for a while; only have a half-dozen head of cattle on the place right now and got them penned and under cover, so I guess we can get the checker game started. You play checkers, gal?"

"I do, but I believe I'll give Momma a hand in the kitchen. I really need to get the recipe for her cobbler. I got a mess of peaches from last summer thawed out and thought I'd make a couple of deep-dish pies."

"You like peaches, gal?" Pa asked.

"I sure do," seeing the grin spreading across his face.

"Well then, kiss my ass; it's a real peach!" and Pa busted out laughing as that was one of his favorite sayings.

"Pa...you ol' fart!" Martha scolded. "What the hell's wrong with you? That's no way to talk to our guest!"

"Hell, I don't know! I guess I was just born thisaway!" and he laughed even harder.

"Don't worry, Momma...there's not much I haven't heard before; let the boys have their fun."

"Yeah, but he don't need to be so crude!" she said as she shook a wooden spoon in Pa's direction.

About that time, a very large dog came meandering into the kitchen from the great room. It was marked like a border collie, black-brown with a white chest but much bigger; he came right up to Terry, laid his head on her thigh, and waited to be petted.

"Pa, would you look at that?"

"What is it?" and he turned to see Terry stroking the dog's head with his eyes closed in contentment.

"I'll be damned! That dog don't take to no one! He's a complete loner; one of the runners dropped him off about a year ago, and he just kinda stuck around."

"He's a sweetheart," and Terry continued to pet his head and scratch his ears. She checked his teeth and said, "He's not that old...four, maybe five years, and he looks really healthy.

A few minutes later, he walked over and drank from a stainless bowl and laid down on an overstuffed, leather-covered, dog bed, "Looks like he's pretty happy here to me."

"Yeah, he's a purdy independent cuss, but he's a great help when it comes to herdin; nothin gets by him!"

By noon, the skies began to clear, and the rain stopped, but the temperature stayed cold. Jasper told Terry to get ready as they had a lot of country to cover in the days to come, and they had better get a move on.

They made a quick tour around the main roads of Missoula to give Terry a basic knowledge of the area that housed the 46-plus thousand folks, and she made more notes on her iPad. Then they turned northeast and caught Highway 89 into the mountains. Jasper was sure they'd hit snow fairly soon, but he was pretty confident that the big Ford with 4-wheel drive would handle it without any problems even with pulling the trailer behind.

"This is quite a rig; can't imagine too many places it won't go," Terry commented.

"Yeah, it's a good one, but don't get overconfident; everything has its limitations. Keep that in mind, and you'll do fine; are you used to driving in snow with a trailer?"

"Yeah...I've been all over the country with my horses and goats for shows in all kinds of weather, so I'm pretty comfortable handling a rig like this."

"Goats?"

"Yes...my darlin pigmy goats; they're precious; like dogs, only cuter."

"You didn't tell me you were a goat-roper."

"You didn't ask; besides, I don't make a habit of roping them, and they produce the best milk you ever tasted. Ever had milk from a pigmy goat?"

"Can't say I have."

"Their milk only has six percent butter fat, and it's so yummy, and my new partner has added some goats to our herd since I've been gone."

"How many do you have?"

"Fifteen does and three bucks, but that number should change come winter; all our does are over a year old, so we should have a pretty good batch of babies around Thanksgiving. Ya know goats can sometimes have three, even four babies at a time, and we already have a pretty good start to our herd. My new partner is a go-getter, and he and his wife are really doing a super job with the farm. I really wasn't looking to sell it as it was my grandpa's, and I grew up there; it's the only home I've ever known, and if everything goes as planned, I'll retire there...that is, unless I get hooked on this country."

"Pay attention...these mountains will grow on ya while yer not even lookin. I originally came here on temporary assignment."

"How long ago was that?"

"Oh, let me see, I guess about 11 years ago now."

"Where'd ya come from?"

"I was born and raised around El Paso, Texas, on a farm in a little town called Anthony on the New Mexico-Texas border; we grew green chilies, onions, and lettuce. My dad tried to rodeo a little but spent more time in the dirt than in the saddle, and his doctor bills always seemed to be more than he won. He's got a case full of belt buckles, but ya can't eat 'em. He made me promise to finish school before I did anything stupid, and I managed to graduate from UTEP in El Paso and get recruited by the Feds before I started rodeoing, thank God!"

"What did you study?"

"Mostly Mexican gals and tequila, but they gave me a degree in business, despite all the partying. Then I spent six months at the FBI academy then came here and been here ever since."

"You ever get back home?"

"Yeah, once or twice a year, usually for the holidays. My folks are fine, and the farm is a money-maker, but I've been away so long that this is home now."

Jasper down-shifted the big rig, and it started to climb. The snow began to blow all around them as they continued up the mountain.

Terry looked over at Jasper, "Have ya got chains?"

"Yeah, got a full set in the trailer, but we should be fine; they've got a half a dozen snow plows that will be out if they're not already. They're always prepared to keep this road clear since it's a main highway. I know all the guys who work for the state, and they're really good guys; you can call them anytime for help if you need to. Get yer phone out, and I'll give you some numbers that could come in handy.

Just then Jasper pulled out his cell and dialed a number, "Buck? Jasper here. What's up, pard? Y'all out workin?"

"Yeah, Jasper! The whole crew is out! What's yer 20?"

"We're about two miles from the crest; what's it like up ahead?"

"It ain't gonna get any better, but I got a plow about three miles ahead of you; you should start seein a clear road in about a mile or so; just take it easy as ya go."

"Roger that, B. How about I buy ya dinner tonight and introduce ya to the new outrider?"

"Sounds like a plan if this storm lets me outta here."

"Alright, buddy; we'll be lookin for ya," and the line went dead.

"Buck Jenson runs the ground crew that keeps I-89 maintained between Missoula and Great Falls, and he and his boys are pretty handy with a smoke wagon too."

"A what?"

"A smoke wagon! Didn't you watch *Tombstone?*" That's a classic line that Kurt Russell said to Billy Bob Thornton. *Go ahead and grab that smoke wagon; go on, grab it and see what happens*; don't tell me you haven't seen that movie."

"Sorry, haven't spent a lot of time watchin movies; there's usually too much to do on the farm."

"Well, then...looks like we got a date for the movies tonight. I got a copy in the trailer. *Tombstone* and *Hidalgo* are my favorites."

"*Hidalgo?*"

"Yeah, the almost-true story of a long-distance rider and his appaloosa. It's outrageous but a great movie! It looks as if our evenings are full for the next few nights."

"Sounds like I have some more schooling comin."

"Yup!"

Jasper could begin to see the road again; the plow had done its job, and the snow was blowing but not sticking, and he took his foot off the gas and let his rig idle as they started down the back side of the rocky mountains.

The weather actually began to clear about halfway down the back side of the mountain, and Terry began to breathe a little easier.

Chapter 4

Jasper pulled into a ranch a couple of miles north of Great Falls and found a spot for the rig, got hooked up, and checked the horses. Terry was coming back from an emergency trip to the farmhouse "necessity room" when she saw Jasper's horses heading out across the field at a full run, riderless, and she panicked.

"What the hell happened?" She screamed as she ran up on Jasper, which took him by surprise.

"What! What's wrong?" he looked all around.

"Your horses are loose!" and she pointed towards the hard-running mounts.

"Nah...they're just gettin some exercise; they'll be back in a couple of minutes," and he turned back to what he was doing.

"Are you sure? They look like they're in panic-mode to me."

"Yeah, I'm purdy sure," and he stood and stretched to his full 6'4" height and then up on his toes.

"Take a look," he said and faced his two ol' nags as he called them. They were making a big circle about 300 yards out and heading back in their direction.

"I guess you've done this before?"

"Once or twice; they love to run, but they know where their food is, too."

By the time Jasper had finished unhooking the trailer and hooking up the electric and water, his two horses were nudging him in the back with their muzzles, letting him know it was time for their dinner.

"Well, I guess you know yer stock pretty well," Terry added as they led the two panting horses to the barn.

"Yeah, when ya spend as much time together as we have, ya get to understanding each other purdy good."

They fed and watered the horses and made sure they were secured in their stalls then headed for the ranch house to say their hellos.

Shortly after dark, Buck Jenson pulled his big Ram 3500 onto the property and parked beside Jasper's Ford. Jasper had the wood-burning BBQ glowing bright orange and ready to burn some cow. He had just placed the seasoned two-inch thick porterhouse steaks on the grill, and they sizzled as the cold meat came within two inches of the coals, and flames shot up as grease from the fat on the outside of the steaks dripped onto the red-hot embers. He dropped some fresh jalapeno peppers wrapped in bacon on the right side of the grill where the fire wasn't quite so intense, and they began to cook at once.

Terry had been busy setting an outside picnic table, and her mind wandered back to the farm and her goats and the Douglass's until the smell of the charring bacon and steaks came rushing into her nostrils, and she was jarred back to reality, "Oh my God does that smell amazing!"

"Thanks, kiddo; would you grab the baked spuds out of the "nukerator" and the rest of the fixins from the icebox please?"

"Absolutely! Anything the chef desires!" she said over her shoulder.

It must be something about the big sky country that makes food taste especially good because each meal she'd had since she arrived had tasted better than the one before, and this one was no exception. She piled some butter, sour cream, sharp cheddar cheese, and a sprinkle of fresh chives on her potato and a splash of Worcester on her slab of beef (Jasper had it floating in fresh creamery butter), and it was pure heaven! Buck had brought a fresh loaf of old-world bread for sopping up the juice and a bottle of pretty good wine, and life was just about perfect.

Thirty minutes later, they were sitting by the grill enjoying its warmth and a cup of joe when Jasper's satellite phone started ringing and bouncing on the table.

"This is Jasper!"

"Hey, J...silence...I've got a half a dozen bad guys on my ass! I'm about three, maybe four, minutes out and could use some back up!"

It was Dusty Rodes, one of the outriders, and he was hell-bent for home as he headed down the mountain with a truckload of hot skins and pelts he had snatched from Mut Jackson and his friends while they were out of camp.

They just managed to catch a glimpse of him as they returned and gave chase.

"Dusty's comin in hot; get ready! Terry would you grab a couple of rifles, shotguns, and some ammo?"

"You got it, Jasper!" and she jumped up and made a beeline for the trailer.

"Bring it on in Dusty; we're ready for ya!"

Just then they saw lights clear the top of the hill, and the big truck flashed its high beams three times to let them know it was him. It looked like Dusty had about a 100-yard lead over the bad guys, and he broad-slid and made the gate with the slimmest of clearance.

He shot across the cattle guard and drove the last quarter mile then slid to a stop behind the trucks belonging to Jasper and Buck.

Terry came busting through the door of the trailer with an arm load of guns and both hands full of boxes of bullets and shotgun shells and set them on the picnic table. Everyone was armed and ready for action as two beat-up old pickups slowed just inside the gate to the ranch, and then both drivers floored their vehicles and they shot forward; their trucks may have looked unkempt, but the engines were ready to run.

Teresa had a .308, bolt-action rifle with a scope. Her rifle had been modified to take a ten-round magazine, and she had a second mag in her coat pocket; she made her way between Jasper's truck and the trailer and took a defensive position.

The two trucks full of bad guys came charging in their direction and when they were about 50 yards out, they split up, and one started around Terry's position.

Just as the old truck on her side was almost parallel with her, she squeezed off a round that hit the driver in the chest; the truck made a hard-left turn and headed for the back of the ranch house, increasing its speed. The two men in the bed saw what was coming and bailed even though they knew it would probably mean their lives at that speed.

The man in the passenger's seat panicked and couldn't undo his seatbelt even though he would have had nowhere to go even if he had freed himself from the truck's grip on him. Seconds later, they crashed into the butane tank and then careened to the left into the back door of the mudroom and on into the kitchen. The butane tank exploded and started a chain reaction that ended with the entire structure going up in a ball of flames.

The other truck that came down Jasper's side was met with gunfire from Jasper and Dusty and a couple of wild shots from Buck who wasn't really into gun fights even though he was ready. He just wished he had practiced more.

The passenger took a round in the shoulder, and one of the bad guys in the bed took a load of buckshot in the head and upper body and broke his neck when he fell backwards out of the truck and landed hard on the ground. He was dead in a matter of minutes.

The old truck dashed on by and then made a big U-turn out around the stables and headed back through the south pasture towards the main road. Dusty headed toward his truck when Jasper called him off, "Let him go! I know who he is and where to find him."

Mut Jackson was visibly shaken; he really wasn't prepared for that kind of a welcome; usually, the wolf cops (as he called them) were on their own and not ready for a firefight, but this escapade had wiped out over half of his gang and cost him thousands in pelts. Needless to say, he was not a happy trapper.

He burst through the rickety old gate that was wired to a dead tree, and dried wood splintered and flew in all directions as they traveled on up the mountain; his shotgun rider was screaming in agony,

"Slow down, ya son of a bitch! Don't cha know I been shot? You're killin me!"

"I might as well kill ya! You won't be of any use to me for quite a while," and Mut thought of where he should bury this pain in the ass as he pulled up to his camp.

Back at the ranch, the manager escaped with just a few scratches and some flash burns. Fortunately, his better half was at her weekly Bunco game at the church in town, and he wasn't looking forward to her coming back home to a house that was no longer standing. He told Jasper he was going into town to get a motel, and he and his bride would be back in the early morning to tend to the stock.

By the time the firemen packed up and left, it was almost midnight. Buck had gone home, and Dusty had unloaded the furs in the barn and was headed to his trailer; he would come back in the morning to help out in any way he could.

Terry looked around at the debris and told Jasper, "Well that was exciting! You sure know how to show a girl a romantic evening; what else do you have planned?"

Jasper rolled his eyes and replied, "I don't know about you, girl, but I'm just about ready for some shut eye. I've got an extra bunk in the trailer, or you can throw a blanket on the ground if ya want."

"A blanket on the ground? Do you know how cold it is out here?"

Jasper took his cell phone from his coat pocket and punched his weather app, "Yep...it's 25 degrees and fallin; should be around 18 by sunup with a windchill of around zero."

"I believe I'll take the bunk, if ya don't mind," Terry said trying to decide if he was joking about her sleeping on the ground.

The extra bunk inside the trailer was a tight squeeze even for her 5'4" frame, but it was warm and comfy once she got settled in, and besides, Jasper definitely had no intention of giving up his extra-long, queen-sized bed. Before Terry could wiggle herself into a spot, Jasper began snoring, and she stared at the ceiling and exhaled, "Perfect!"

Chapter 5

The next morning, they both hit the floor at the same time: about fifteen minutes before daylight. Terry was actually surprised she had gotten some rest as she wasn't sure if the child-sized bunk would afford her comfort.

They were just about to sit down with their first cup of joe when the ranch foreman and his wife came driving in. Jasper motioned for them to join Terry and him for some coffee, and he made room at the small table inside the trailer for them and poured two more cups of coffee. The rancher's wife shed a few tears as they drank and talked about the previous night's loss of their home.

"I spoke with Jerry Abbott last night," Jasper told them, "And there should be a contractor and some workers here before noon to start planning the rebuild of the ranch house. So sorry about all the mess."

"Wow...that's some service!" the rancher's wife said.

"This is a purdy important place for us outriders, so I think you'll be impressed with the new house, and y'all need to move to the best hotel in town till it's done."

"Are you sure? There's some pretty fancy places around these parts," said the rancher.

"I know, but yer gonna be holed up for six months or more, so ya need to be comfortable, and ya need to start shopping for clothes and furniture and whatever else you will need. You'll find Mr. Abbott to be a very sympathetic and easy man to work with, and he will want you to have the very best."

After the rancher and his wife left, Jasper and Terry saddled up the horses and took them for a short ride before they loaded them into the trailer and headed off for the 30-minute or so trip to where Dusty Rodes had his trailer parked.

Mut Jackson was tired of being a nursemaid to his wounded associate, and around five o'clock in the morning after his latest screaming session about needing a hospital, Mut pulled his Ruger .44 magnum out of his belt, and as the man's eyes got big as saucers, Mut put a round into his head that almost made it disintegrate as his associate flew backwards and smashed to the ground outside. Then Mut turned very nonchalantly and walked back to his dilapidated shack, laid down on his cot, and drifted off to sleep like nothing had even happened.

Terry, Jasper, and Dusty headed up the mountain on horseback. They each had foul weather gear on and plenty of ammunition and supplies, enough to last them for several days. Jasper knew where to locate Mut Jackson's camp, but it had been 16 hours since the confrontation at the ranch, and there was no telling where or what could have happened in that amount of time.

They rode through the broken-down gate just as the sun began to set, and the temperature began to drop. Before long, they spotted Mut's rundown old cabin and truck about a 100 yards down the road. They rode passed what looked like a partially covered body laying just off the dirt road, which reminded Jasper of fresh road-kill.

There was no smoke coming from the cabin, which was strange based on the weather. They spread out and approached the cabin with caution as each one had their hand gun at the ready. By the time they had secured the area and checked the body, it was darker than the inside of a cow, and Jasper suggested they spend the night in the cabin since it seemed to be vacated and get a fresh start down the mountain come morning.

In the cabin, Terry found fresh water and cookware and made coffee, beef, and beans that were considerably better than the two men were used to when they were on the trail; they rearranged the inside of the cabin as they looked through everything they could find and put their bedrolls on the cots that were located around the three-room shack with Terry getting a room to herself.

After they were settled, Jasper used the satellite phone to contact Jerry Abbott and made his report. He told him there was no sign of Mut, but he left them a body to deal with. Then he mentioned they would continue their chase early in the morning after they took pictures of the dead man outside; the cleanup crew would have to deal with the body, and Jasper assured him that he was positive he knew where Mut was headed.

The next morning before sunup, the three outriders ate some more beef and beans and drank some left-over coffee, took photographs of the dead man, then headed down the mountain and back toward their rigs.

Jasper moved his horses in close beside Terry, and after a few minutes he said, "You did a really good job back at the ranch the other night. I meant to say something several times before now, but things kept getting in the way, and I forgot."

"Thanks, but you didn't have to say anything."

"I know, but it's easy to say something when ya screw up but sometimes we just forget to let ya know when ya do good, and you did good!"

"Well, thank you."

"Have you ever killed a man before?"

"No, I haven't, not till now."

"Have you ever blown up a house before?"

"No...can't say I've done that either."

"Well," Jasper said; "All I can say is yer off to one hell of a start!" and they both laughed out loud.

When they got back to their rigs, Jasper talked to Abbott on the satellite phone as they drove northeast on Highway 87 toward Ft. Benton, a sleepy little town of about 1500 people located on the Missouri River 25 or 30 miles from their location.

Mut Jackson was sitting on a stool with a draft beer and a shot in front of him. The Pastime Bar, a couple of blocks off the river, was not a place for tourists. Blondie the bartender and waitress was not a real blonde, even 30 years ago before she turned completely gray and stopped coloring her hair on a regular basis. The fact that the Pastime Bar was not where she planned to be at 72 years of age spoke volumes about her attitude, and she would let anybody know that in a New York minute; nobody in their right mind crossed Blondie unless they were anxious to deal with a knife or gun or just get escorted out the door.

For Blondie, the job wasn't just about making money; it was about getting through the day with as few reminders of her station in life as possible, and the clientele who frequented the bar did nothing to help her forget.

Mut was the first person through the door at 8:30 in the morning after Blondie opened up. Two more old regulars sauntered in and were at their spots by 9 a.m. The Pastime served food when Blondie was in the mood to fix a burger, a plate of scrambled eggs, or a PB&J sandwich, but mostly the regulars just ate the free peanuts and brushed the shells off the bar onto the floor, and the night bartender sorted through the forgotten, discarded peanut shells with a garden rake a couple of times a week if he was of a mind, which helped to pass the time.

Mut was still totally pissed off over losing his furs, his trucks, and his men, a couple of which he actually cared about, but obviously not the one he had put a bullet in the day before or even the last one who ran off shortly after they hit Ft. Benton. Now, he figured he would have to find a new base of operations because he was positive the FEDs had been there and found the body, and well shit, things had just turned to crap for him in the in the last 36 hours, unfortunately for him. Little did he know that this bar would be the last place he would ever see.

Chapter 6

Terry and Jasper had stopped at a hamburger joint about five miles out of town for some coffee and information. Ruby May, their waitress, was famous in those parts for knowing everything that went on.

When they walked in, Ruby May came right over to their table and leaned down a bit, so Jasper could get a little peek at her cleavage.

"Jasper...you good-lookin sumbitch, where you been, honey? Ain't seen you in weeks!" she said with all the enthusiasm she could muster, ignoring Terry and Dusty in the process.

"Hey, Ruby! How ya doin, gal?" Jasper said with much less enthusiasm than Ruby but with a crooked grin on his face.

"Well...the only way I'd be doin any better is if I had yer long, lanky, body in my bed fer a couple of hours!" and they all laughed, well, all except Terry who just smiled politely and gave Ruby May a looking over. Terry noticed that Ruby May was well-built, but there were signs of being "rode pretty hard," and it was difficult for Terry to get a feel for her age. She figured Ruby was somewhere between 35 and 60, and Terry thought that she might be being kind in that estimation.

Jasper continued to grin up at her, "We're lookin fer Mut Jackson; any sign of him around?"

"Well," she stopped and looked at her watch. "If it were me, and I really wanted to put my hands on him, I'd start at the Pastime Bar, and I'd be very careful cuz he's in a real bad mood, and he's got that big .44 on his hip. He was here fer ham and eggs about seven this mornin."

"What's he wearin, kiddo?"

"That maroon wool shirt he always wears and a black leather coat with a black ball cap. He's *very* color coordinated, don't cha know? I think the cap had *Don't Mess with Texas* embroidered in red and blue lettering on the front, but don't quote me on that."

"That's fine, girl! That tells me what we need to know; how about a couple cups of yer famous joe?"

"Sure! Anything to eat?" she asked as she started to walk away.

"No, thanks, doll-face; we're good," he said as she walked away.

She turned around and said as an afterthought, "Oh yeah, he was drivin a late-model Ram 1500 truck; white I think; it was kinda dirty, if ya know what I mean?" The she hurried off to grab their coffee.

"She seems nice!" Terry said with a half smirk on her face, and Jasper could feel the sarcasm without even looking up, which made him grin a little.

"Yeah, Ruby was one of the first people I met when I moved to the big sky; we've been friends for years, and if ya need to know anything about anything in a 200-square mile area, Ruby's the go-to person. Got it?"

"Yeah, I got it!" Terry said just as Ruby set two oversized cups of steaming coffee in front of them that smelled heavenly.

Once Jasper and Terry were back in Jasper's truck, he began to lay out the plan to get Mut. He discussed where he was going to leave his rig, what the inside of the Pastime bar looked like, and how they were going in to get Mut.

Outside the Pastime Bar, Terry pulled the heavy handle on the backdoor, and it gave way. Jasper had said that it would be unlocked, and he was right.

She walked stealthily into the kitchen, which didn't look like it had seen much use lately and made her way to the swinging doors that allowed her to see the full length of the 40-foot bar with three customers seated. Mut Jackson was seated in the middle with four or five empty stools on each side of him.

Terry pushed the #1 speed dial on her cell phone, heard it ring once, and hung up; five seconds later, Jasper came through the front door with his gun hanging down in his right hand, and Terry stepped through the swinging doors and stood at the ready with her Glock 26 charged and ready just as Jasper shouted out,

"Mut Jackson! Federal agents! Yer under arrest! Put yer hands above yer head and don't do anything stupid because I'd just as soon shoot cha as mess with yer useless carcass!"

Terry almost laughed out loud as she listened to Jasper's patter. It was almost like being in the Old West.

Mut Jackson was taken completely by surprise. His head snapped up from his drink, and as he looked for the voice, his hand automatically went down for his .44 magnum.

"Don't do it, Mut! It won't end good for ya!" Jasper yelled.

"Ah, bullshit!" Mut mumbled as he pulled out the big magnum, and Terry knew it was about to get ugly.

Just as Mut's gun cleared the rail of the bar, Jasper fired, and Terry followed suit. Two of Jasper's slugs hit Mut under his left arm, and one of Terry's hit him between his right eye and ear, and he began to fall to his left side toward the floor.

Unfortunately, before he went down, he had thumbed back the hammer on the big gun, and his index finger squeezed as he fell; the large single-action gun exploded, and a .44 slug hit the unsuspecting Blondie square in the chest, right between the very un-voluptuous cleavage of her 72-year old breasts, bringing to conclusion the worry about what she would do to solve her choice of professions. She went airborne as the very large slug raised her thin, bony body up and backward into the rack of half-full bottles of alcohol, and they all came crashing down on top of

Blondie's multicolored hair and then all around her as she bled out on the cement floor behind the bar.

"What about Mut's remaining accomplice?" Terry asked.

"He'll turn up. He's not the sharpest knife in the drawer, and there's not a lot he can do at this point in his career 'cept maybe apply for a job at McDonald's. Last I heard, they still do some background checks, so he maybe screwed there, too." Jasper said with a grin, "But no matter, 'Mickey-Dees' will hire anyone."

Several days later, Jerry Abbott's corporate jet flew Terry through the frigid sky back home towards Joplin, Missouri, to get back and pick up her new truck and trailer and then head back to Montana to her new life and adventure.

Chapter 7

L arry and Kathy Douglass had been hard at work the entire time that Terry had been on the road, and the farm looked visibly better than the last time she was home. How was that even possible?

Terry took two days to load out her new rig and get used to the layout. She loaded Biscuit and Gravy in and out several times and then took them on several short road trips to get them used to their new surroundings.

At first light on one beautiful, spring morning, Terry put her 30-ounce insulated steel mug in the cup holder of her new truck, hugged Larry and Kathy, then headed for Montana.

Terry had targeted Omaha, Nebraska, for her first stop. Her truck's GPS read 5 hours and 21 minutes, and she figured another hour or so on top of that because she was still getting used to the new rig. Nevertheless, she hit the city limits on Interstate 29 at exactly 11 a.m. She guessed she could figure it right on the nose from then on.

She stopped, filled up with diesel, gave the horses a snack, and checked their water then hit the "gym" (her word for the ladies' room). The word made her smile because she didn't have to worry about a workout for the day. Then she got back on the road. It was three hours and 17 minutes to Sioux Falls, South Dakota. Then she made a left-hand turn onto I-90 west; she thought about stopping for nourishment, but she was so excited about being on the road that hunger was not even a problem at that moment.

The Pine Ridge Indian Reservation, home of the Oglala Sioux, housed close to 40,000 on 2.8 million acres, which made it the second largest Reservation in the United States and the second poorest county in the states as well. There, the average income per capita was $6,286 but over 4.5 million cans of beer were sold annually in White Clay, Nebraska, just over the border from Pine Ridge because the rest of the county was dry. That amounted to more than 12,500 cans of beer a day sold, four times the average amputations and deaths due to diabetes than the average U.S. population.

Teresa was painfully aware of those statistics and being almost full-blooded Indian, she wished there was something she could do to motivate her people to take better care of themselves, but she also knew it had been going on for way too long by that point, and her people were probably too set in their ways to change.

She found a roadside park and unloaded her horses. She rode Biscuit bareback and lead Gravy by the lead rope, and all three worked the stiffness out together. After a mile or so, she returned to the rig and tied the two horses back in the woods out of sight.

She fed and watered her stock then settled down for the evening. She fixed a bowl of Ramen in the microwave with a tall glass of Crown Reserve on ice, and she drifted off to sleep as she stretched out on the couch with her clothes on.

She thought she heard something in the middle of the night and got up to check with her Glock in hand, but after a thorough look around, she found nothing and headed back to her space. This time her queen-sized bed called her name, and sleep came easy.

At just before sunup the next morning, she took the horses for another short ride then loaded, fed, and watered them and headed on west. From the Bad Lands of South Dakota to Helena was about 11 hours and some change, and Terry was beginning to feel the fatigue of the time on the road alone.

She decided not to try and make it all the way that day and to find a place to hole up and do the last couple of hours in the morning. She drove hard and only stopped for gas and a quick sandwich at McDonalds' and checked the horses. Then she was back on the road.

The last stop of the day was Butte, and she parked at the back of the parking lot of Carlson's Steak House where their sign read *Best Meat in Montana*. She decided they were going to have to prove that because she'd had some pretty dang good beef in the last several weeks riding around with Jasper. Her steak was really good, but it was a far cry from being the *best* in Montana.

She was just finishing her meal when a scraggly old cowboy stepped up beside her booth and tried to start a conversation.

"How ya doin dollface? Lookin fer some company?"

"Nope! Just passin through," was her reply without looking up as she had already seen him coming out of the corner of her eye.

"Why don't cha slide over, and I'll buy ya...ah..." he looked the table over, "another cup of coffee?"

"Why don't you go mind yer own business and we'll both be fine," she replied.

"Aww, don't be thata way, purdy thing; ya know ya want some company."

"Maybe so, but not yours," and she looked up into his dark eyes without blinking and held her stare. After a couple of seconds, he seemed to get the picture.

"Well, I guess that's just yer bad luck then, missy!"

"Yeah, I guess so, but I'll deal with it."

He tipped his hat and smiled, trying not to look like the fool everyone in the place knew he was, and he walked away.

Fifteen minutes later, Terry was checking her horses to make sure they had feed and water when a hand landed on her left shoulder, and she pulled her Glock 26 with her right hand and let it hang at her side, "You are an even bigger fool than you act like!" She spun to her left, and there was another dumb-looking cowboy standing behind the first, "Oh, and it looks you have a twin brother."

"Hey...you should learn to be nicer to people!"

"And you should learn to recognize the Law when you see it!"

His eyes snapped open.

"I'm a Federal agent!" and she pulled her coat aside with her left hand to expose the silver and gold badge hanging on her wide belt.

The cowboy knew he was in trouble but wasn't smart enough to figure out what to do about it. Instead of just backing away, he started to pull a skinning knife from the sheath on his belt, but to no avail. Terry brought her right hand up from her side and hit him with all her might in the right side of his head with the full impact of her Glock and a ten-round magazine, and his eyes fluttered then rolled back into his head as he headed for the ground like a toe sack full of spuds.

Just before he settled, she put a well-placed, size eight, cowboy boot in his groin. He didn't feel it then, but he certainly would when he woke up.

The slow-minded cowpoke behind him was having trouble processing the whole thing and decided to pull his own knife and join the party. He took one step in Terry's direction, and she pulled the slide on her Glock and let a round slam home and put a .9mm round in his right thigh, which caused him to scream in pain, and he went down on the blacktop, dropping his knife. Just as she was about to massage his *huevos* with her boot, a voice called out, "Drop the gun and put yer hands in the air!"

"Federal agent on the job!" she called back.

"Don't move! Show me some ID!"

"Badge on my belt!"

"With yer left hand, slowly pull yer coat aside."

Terry did as she was instructed, and the tension started to ease.

"Everything ok, Sheriff?"

"I'm not a sheriff! I'm a state trooper."

"Yes, sir, Sheriff, I understand," she said, and he realized she was having a little fun with him.

She replaced the spent round in her magazine and place the Glock back in the hand-tooled holster on her right hip as they talked.

"Did you identify yourself as a Federal agent?"

"Not inside the restaurant, but as soon as he put his hands on me, I did, and I guess he panicked. He could have walked away, and I would have let him be, but he made the wrong decision by pulling out his knife."

"I see; I would have done the same thing. You can be on your way."

"Thanks, Sheriff," she said with a grin and got into her truck and pulled out of the parking lot back onto the highway.

By 8:00 p.m., she found a roadside park and had her horses out and moving down a moonlit trail. They were gone about an hour, and fatigue was starting to set into her body. However, she was getting used to her living quarters and looking forward to her queen-sized bed.

About 15 minutes before sun up seemed to be the normal time for her to rise. She showered and dressed in clean Wranglers and a white George Strait western shirt and brushed the dust off her boots, fed and watered her stock, and hit the road for Helena about an hour northeast up I-15. She finally reached her destination not the worse for wear.

Sitting in Jerry Abbott's office, Terry's mind drifted while he finished his phone call. She thought of Jasper and the Douglass's back on the farm, about the goats and the two cowboys she had to put in their places. Finally, Mr. Abbott spoke, pulling her back to reality,

"So...Terry my dear, how was your trip?"

"Long, tiring, and relatively uneventful, sir," she said.

"Do you call putting two saddle tramps in the hospital uneventful?"

"Uh, no, sir! I guess that slipped my mind; they weren't really any threat, just a couple of guys with too much Colorado Kool-Aid under their belts."

"Well, I gotta say, I sure like yer ability to compartmentalize things. By the way, Jasper rounded up Mut Jackson's sidekick, and it didn't turn out well for him; he won't need to worry about his next job; it's probably gonna be stoking the furnaces of hell. He tried to resist, and Jasper had to put him down."

"Yes, sir," she responded, but she was already aware of the situation as she and Jasper talked at least twice a day everyday while she had been gone. She liked hearing his voice every day and looked forward to his calls, and he was making sure her training continued.

"Get some rest at the ranch, and then tomorrow you need to head toward East Glacier Park. There are signs of poachers working on the bear population out on the Blackfoot Reservation; we've had reports of carcasses being found with bullet holes in them."

"Yes, sir."

"You can hook up with Jasper tomorrow evening. He's on his way from down south as we speak; make sure you have plenty of supplies; no tellin how long you'll be out in the hills, if ya know what I mean."

"Yes, sir. I'm beginning to get a feel for what's going on up here under the big sky."

Abbott just smiled and waved her off.

"Stay in touch, Miss Littrel, and stay alive. I'm starting to take a liking to ya."

"I'll do my best, sir."

The ranch was about a 30-minute drive north west up I-287; the destination was plugged into Terry's GPS, and it would have been easy to miss with all the trees and vegetation along the highway. The well-kept road led her back about a quarter of a mile until she came to a large gate hung on huge logs about 18 feet tall with one across the top and a hand-carved sign about four feet high and eight feet wide that read *Flying G* along with a big G with wings on the right side.

She found the camping area about 35 or 40 yards from the main house and pulled into the first available space and stepped out and stretched; she heard Biscuit and Gravy stomping their hooves on the floor of the trailer and decided they needed some exercise before anything else, so she unloaded them and hopped up on Biscuit and lead Gravy by the reigns down a little trail.

She was getting used to riding bareback as she did it a lot as a young girl on the farm but had changed her ways some as she got older; however, being in better shape and spending more time with her horses seemed to make it a natural thing to do, and it was quicker and easier than saddling them up.

The meadow at the back of the large log cabin ran up toward the forest, and Terry headed in that direction. As she passed the back of the main house, a nice-looking woman waved her over, and she reigned Biscuit in that direction.

"Miss Littrel, I have hot coffee and an apple pie waiting for you when you get back, and you can take any of the empty stalls for your stock. Hope you enjoy yer ride!" and she waved once again.

The inside of the main house was much like the others she had stayed at: lots of western decor, heavy leather furniture with Indian blankets folded over the backs and lots of trophies hanging on the wall that happened to be some of the biggest elk and ram trophies she had ever seen. There were also mountain lions and wolves that lined the walls and a giant fireplace with a rock chimney that ran all the way to the ceiling, close to 18 or 20 feet would be her guess, and there was a roaring fire already going in the fireplace. Terry felt like she could lay down under a blanket and sleep for a week.

The house mom, Mary Munday, was as friendly as she was nice-looking, and it wasn't long before the two were laughing in deep conversation over a giant slice of Dutch apple pie and a huge cup of really good joe.

"Mary, are you all alone here?" Terry couldn't find any sign of a man inside the big home.

"Oh, hell no, sweetie! I got half a dozen horses and some cattle that are recouping, and ya never know what the riders are gonna bring through the gate; every day's a surprise, but I ain't never alone!"

"Seems like a big job for a woman," and then Terry realized that her comment didn't sound very complimentary. "I'm sorry...I didn't mean that you weren't capable. I just meant...oh hell...you know what I meant, right?"

"Don't worry about it, Miss Littrel. I learned a long time ago that men are fun to have around, but I sure as hell don't need one to take care of me, or worse yet, for me to take care of him," and they both laughed out loud.

"It's Terry, and I know exactly what you mean!" she replied.

"It should get down into the teens tonight, and the spare bedroom has got a brand-spanking new king-sized bed with a goose-feather comforter on it, so make yerself at home if yer a mind!"

"Why thank you, Mary, I just might do that."

They played checkers and visited till close to midnight, and Terry enjoyed one of the best night's sleep she could remember in a long while.

When she hit the floor just before sunup, she smelled fresh coffee and something baking in the oven; by the time she got to the kitchen, Mary was coming through the backdoor shaking the snow off her wide brimmed hat, and the shoulders of her heavy sheepskin coat had about a quarter of an inch of snow built up on them as well.

"Mornin, girlfriend! It's really comin down out there! I gave yer stock some good feed and put their covers on them; nice couple of cayuses you got there."

"Thanks, Mary. They're family, if ya know what I mean? They've been with me since they were just a few months old."

Terry handed her a large cup of coffee, and they both drank with their eyes closed enjoying the warmth of the stout brew; then Mary removed a large sheet pan from the oven with about a dozen of the biggest cinnamon rolls Terry had ever seen, and they smelled wonderful.

"I know things are big in Texas, but I think Montana must be right beside 'em: the steaks, spuds, pie, and rolls are crazy good and large as well!"

"Yeah, well it only takes a little bit longer to do it right!"

Just about that time, the satellite phone rang, and Mary answered it.

"Hey, Jasper...where you at, darlin?" she listened as he filled her in on his plan. "Got it, kiddo! I'll hold her here till I see yer smilin face."

"Jasper's a couple hours out, maybe even longer with this weather; he wants you to hang around till he gets here. Then y'all can decide on yer next move. Looks like we got some checkers to be played."

"Looks to me like we got some rolls to eat first," Terry said, and they laughed.

Three and a half hours later, Jasper crept slowly over the cattle guard and into the space next to Terry's rig. The snow was falling even harder than it was at sunup, and Jasper was glad to be off the road and safe for the time being. He knew that anyone trying to make a run for it would end up in a ditch or off the side of the mountain, and he'd still find them, sooner or later.

He unloaded his horses and put them in a stable with freshwater and good grain and a blanket over each one. Then he made a dash for the coffee and cinnamon rolls that he knew were waiting for him inside.

Mary and Terry had a large mug of coffee and a platter of rolls out on the counter as Jasper busted through the back door.

"Dang, ladies! It's like winter time out there! I reckon we better hunker down here till it breaks," and he looked at Terry.

"You got my attention, cowboy. I can't think of a better place to wait out a storm," and they came together and hugged.

They separated, and Jasper looked down into Terry's eyes, "How was yer trip, young lady?"

"Uneventful," she replied, blushing a little.

"You mean except for shooting a cowboy and putting both him and his partner in the hospital, right?"

"Uh...yeah! Hell, does everyone in the state know about that?"

Mary piped up, "Uh...I don't! I guess you neglected to tell me you were shootin folks on the way across the country when you came in," she said with a slight grin.

"It's not really that big of a deal. They were just a couple ol' boys that couldn't keep their hands to themselves, and anyway, they'll survive, unfortunately."

They all had a good laugh and sat down and had rolls and coffee and to Terry, life seemed very good, at least for the moment.

Chapter 8

After two days of taking care of their horses, sitting in front of the fireplace in overstuffed leather chairs, eating great food, listening to classic country music, and catching up on their rest, it didn't take long for Terry and Jasper to get restless.

By the third day, the clouds were gone, and Jasper checked that the roads were clear. He decided they should be on their way towards East Glacier Park.

Terry figured it would be about a three-hour drive if the roads remained clear and there were no accidents along the way. The weather was just above freezing, but there was still lots of black ice on the road where there was shade from the tall trees close to the highway, and Jasper kept calling and reminding Terry not to oversteer or hit her brakes too hard and land in a ditch, "Yes, sir, boss! Got it boss!" and she could her Jasper's sighs on the other end of the line.

His reply was a little terse, "I ain't yer boss! I'm just here to help ya clear up this mess cause yer a proby, and we wouldn't want cha gettin in over yer head, got it?"

"Yes, sir, boss!" and the line went dead. A few seconds later, Terry crossed a bridge on a downgrade and hit a patch of black ice and started to slide to the right, and she thought, "Damn it, Terry! Pay attention!" and even though she was getting close to the right side of the road and a steep drop off, she turned the wheel to the right and the big rig came out of the slide, and she corrected back into her lane without incident.

Two seconds later, her satellite phone rang, go figure, "Yes, my dear...what is it now?" she asked.

"What the hell was that? Didn't I just tell you not two minutes ago to pay attention?"

"Not a problem, love. I just dropped my cigarette in my lap, and well...you know."

"Cigarette? You don't even smoke! What the hell are you talkin about?"

Terry could hear the anger and concern in his voice, and it kind of made her smile although she really hadn't meant to upset her new best friend.

Three hours and fifteen minutes after they hit the road, they pulled into the village of East Glacier Park. The city limits sign read, *Welcome to Glacier Park! Population 363,* but that was in 2010, and the sign was full of bullet holes and just about rusted through in most places.

Jasper called Terry's phone again, "There's a public parking lot on the left on the next block and a purdy good soup kitchen across the street."

"I'll follow you," she said and pulled into an almost empty lot that looked like it would hold a 150 or more cars. She checked her instruments on the dash, and the temp outside was 29, and the wind was starting to blow ice pellets sideways. She slipped into her wool-lined coat, cranked her hat down on her head and fell in behind Jasper as they made their way to *Shotgun Sam's Home-cookin.*

When they walked in, the owner yelled, "Jasper, how the hell ya doin, pard? Saw ya pull into the lot. Who's this purdy little thang?"

"Good to see ya, Sam. This is Terry Littrel, the new outrider," and they shook hands as Sam looked her up and down.

"My, my! I can't wait fer her to come back, and she ain't even left yet." Terry almost blushed, and the two men laughed.

"Ya got any fresh barbeque?" Jasper asked.

"Got the hind end of an elk that just came out of the smoker and some beans and biscuits ifin yer interested."

"Whaddaya think. Miss T?"

"I don't know what yer gonna eat because I could eat the hind end of an elk all by myself!" and Sam chimed in, "I truly like this little gal."

"Sam, what do ya know about the carcasses they been findin up on the Res?"

"There's been some strangers in and out of town every couple weeks for the last month or so. They drive a big old truck all jacked up with dual wheels and pullin a trailer, shouldn't be hard to spot this time of year. I couldn't say for sure they're the folks yer lookin for, but it sure wouldn't surprise me none. The forest rangers asked about 'em a while back, but I haven't seen them lately, now that I think about it."

The two finished eating some of the best smoked meat Terry had ever tasted and then downed a bowl of peach cobbler covered in heavy cream and another cup of Sam's good coffee.

Terry said, "That should hold me for a while," and Sam smiled a semi-toothless smile.

"You come on back, Miss Terry; you can bet I'll be waitin fer ya! Be careful up on that mountain, ya hear?"

"I hear ya, Sam. Thanks, will do!"

Terry fell in behind Jasper as they headed up the mountain on a poorly maintained black-top road. The sun was beginning to come out from behind the clouds, and the ice was starting to breakup under the tires of the two rigs as Jasper led them up the road to the Blackfoot stronghold.

They pulled into side-by-side campsites and found that only four other spaces were occupied, one that held a big Ram 3500 with a trailer similar to theirs.

"Let's go over to the trading post and see what we can find out," and Jasper led the way as the ice crunched beneath his boots. Terry followed in his footsteps to keep from slipping on the frozen ground.

Gary Greywing worked at the Reservation store and made just enough to heat his one-room shack and buy his beer. He looked up as the two walked in, "Hey Jasper! What are you doin out in weather like this?"

"Hey, Gary...just takin care of business. I would like you to meet Terry Littrel, the new outrider," and she and Gary shook hands and smiled.

Terry noticed the 30-something Indian looked swollen and unhealthy, a look that was prevalent throughout the Reservation.

"What can you tell us about that big rig in space number 13 out there, Gary?"

"Couple of palefaces drive it. They been here for five or six weeks. They bought fishing licenses and tags for a deer or two, but they come and go, mostly at night and don't seem to bother anybody."

"You have any idea where they stay when they're not here in camp?"

"Naah! I never really pay much attention to them, I guess."

"What about the rangers? Where have they been, lately?"

"Not sure. I haven't seen them for a while, either."

"Gary, would you call me if the rangers come back? I need to talk to them, and please let me know if those campers come back around."

"Sure, Jasper. If I see anybody, I'll let ya know for sure!"

"Thanks, pard!"

Terry and her partner headed for their rigs to unload their horses and prepare them for a long ride and the possibility of harsh weather.

"Do ya think we can count on Gary?" she asked.

"If he's sober when they come back to camp, he'll call, and that's about all I can tell ya. Let's go over and check out their rig."

They stopped and ground-reined their horses while they checked out the campers' horse trailer. It was empty and no recent sign of any animals being in there.

"Looks like they're on foot. I wonder what the inside of the camper looks like?" and Jasper pulled a set of lock picks from the rear pocket of his Wranglers.

"Do you have a warrant?" Terry asked with a smile on her face, and Jasper just grunted as the lock released, and the trailer door swung open. They stepped inside, and the smell of rotting flesh filled their nostrils. They saw 15 or 20 grey wolf pelts and two or three brown bear skins that were folded and stacked on the bunk. They had been partially tanned, just enough to make them portable, but the stench from inside the sleeping area of the trailer was very intense.

"Looks like we found our folks," Jasper stated.

"Looks like it!" Terry agreed.

Biscuit and Gravy were both excited to be out of the trailer and on solid ground even though it was cold as all get out. Terry could feel their excitement, and she felt much the same as they rode down the trail.

"I know a couple of spots where they might be holed up in this weather, which could make it a little easier to corral them," Jasper stated.

"I'm with you, big man; let's go get 'em and stop this senseless slaughter."

It was getting late in the afternoon, almost three, and the temperature was beginning to drop, "I hope yer not planning on sleeping on the ground tonight, cowboy."

"It could happen, but there's a cabin a mile or so up the trail that we keep stocked just for times like this; unless the bad guys have taken it over, we should have a warm bed and some hot grub tonight. Tomorrow could be a different story, though."

When they reached the cabin that Jasper had spoken of, they put their horses into the makeshift stall and gave them hay and water and took their tac into the cabin to keep it from freezing stiff.

"Cozy!" Terry said as she looked around the one-room shack. Against one wall, three army cots were folded up to make room to walk around the small interior. Terry found a can of black beans and took some turkey jerky from her pack and added some rice and spices and put it all together on top of a one-burner camp stove in the corner of the room. Thirty minutes later, they had a bowel of pretty good chili. She drug out her bottle of Tabasco and doused her dinner and then passed it on to Jasper .

"What would we do without Avery Island's finest?" he asked.

"Yep!" Terry added. "I can get by without a lot of things like clean socks and underwear, but I'd be a mess without my Tabasco."

"Underwear? I didn't think you wore underwear," he said with a sly grin.

"What would make you think that?" she asked.

"Oh...just a feeling I got!"

"Well...I don't, but if I did...uh...what was the question? And...how the hell did we get to talkin about my underwear, or lack thereof?"

Jasper couldn't help but smile, "Well, it is something I've found myself thinkin about from time to time here lately."

"What?" she asked.

"You without any underwear."

Terry started to blush just a bit and took another bite of makeshift chili, so it hopefully wouldn't show.

The small cabin was fitted with the bare necessities, but it definitely was not a deluxe room at the Hilton, not quite heated to the max, so Terry and Jasper kept their heavy coats on until it was time to slip into their sleeping bags.

"This place is only just a little better than sleeping outside; it hasn't been very long, but I'm already spoiled, and I miss my trailer."

Jasper smiled, "Yeah, I know what ya mean. I'm really attached to my queen-sized bunk."

"Where do you suppose those bad guys are hold up?" Terry asked.

"Well, there's a cave about two miles from here up the north trail; not too many folks are aware of it, but it would be good enough to keep a couple of bad guys out of the weather."

After they finished their meal, they both slipped into their sleeping bags and fell asleep at once.

Chapter 9

The next morning two hours before sunup, Terry heard Jasper moving around the small structure, "Are you going to sleep tonight?" she asked.

"Umm...it's morning, and we need to get a jump on those guys up ahead of us, so get yer lazy, no under-wearing butt out of that sack, and let's get started!"

"What's the weather like?" she asked.

"Let's just say ya may want to put on everything ya got and hope it's enough; it snowed again late last night. I'm gonna bring the horses down from the stable, so we can saddle them here and keep the tac warm; go ahead and get dressed and put on a pot of joe while yer at it, if you please?"

"Yes, sir! Got it!" and she could tell the room temperature was not going to be very comfortable when she crawled out of her bedroll. Fortunately, Terry had spent enough time in the cold weather camping and riding that she was prepared for what was to come.

Two large cups of steaming coffee and some jerky, and it was time to saddle up and head on up the mountain to try and surprise the poachers.

Two miles away, up the north trail, huddled down in a small cave not quite high enough for either man to stand and stretch to his full height, Rance Martin kicked his companion in the butt, "Hey! It's snowin out! I think we'll just hunker down in here till it breaks."

"Great! So why the hell did ya have to wake me then?"

"I just thought you'd like to know."

Rance really didn't care too much for his trapping buddy. He was just someone to help tote the pelts down the mountain, and Rance was figuring that the idiot may not make it all the way back to the trailer, depending on how many furs they ended up with.

Terry and Jasper traveled about a mile or so in the darkness on horseback; the snow had let up, but Terry had no idea of where they were going. She had never been in the area before, and if it weren't for the snow covering the trail, she could have used her laptop to guide her, but Jasper actually knew the trail, so they continued on at a slow pace.

Terry raised her hand, and they both pulled up their horses.

"What is it?" Jasper whispered.

"I just got a whiff of campfire," she said.

A few seconds later, Jasper said, "Yeah! I got it. They're right where I figured they'd be. We'll ride another quarter mile or so; then we'll go the last little bit on foot."

"Whatever you say, boss!"

Terry was dealing with the cold and didn't want to make too many decisions on her own.

Poaching was a hard profession. It was smelly and dirty, and the poacher was always hiding out looking over his or her shoulder to make sure the law wasn't close by, not to mention sleeping on the ground most of the time and hanging with some not so smart people. But most of all, poaching could get a person killed.

"How did ya know they'd be in this cave?" Terry asked.

"We've staked these caves out, and anyway, poachers aren't exactly rocket scientists. I can't tell you how many we've caught just hangin out like this."

Just before they pulled their guns, Terry heard the crying of a small animal, either a coyote or a wolf pup, but she ignored its cry for help and went on as there were other things to take care of first.

"I'm gonna go over the top of the cave and get on the other side of the opening. Stay down until I'm in position. Then I'll call out and give them a chance to surrender."

"Got it, boss!"

Terry took cover as Jasper headed up and over the side of the mountain that housed the cave entrance. Fifteen minutes later, she saw Jasper pop his head up from behind a boulder and give her the high sign.

"Hey...you in the cave! U.S. Federal Agents! We know yer in there, and that you have illegal pelts; we're not going to ask you twice to come out with your hands up! Do it now! You have ten seconds to comply!"

The first shots came out of the cave with no purpose; they hit a couple of trees, and snow fell from their branches. Terry and Jasper opened up with their rifles both bouncing rounds off the inside wall of the cave from their positions. They had fired three rounds each when they heard a scream come from within.

"Oh shit! Damn it!"

"Yer not taking us alive!" came another voice from the cave.

"That's ok with us!" Jasper yelled back and fired off two more rounds.

"I don't want to die in this smelly ol' cave! I need a doc cuz I'm hit purdy good!"

Rance Martin looked at his companion laying on the ground, "Yeah, well, it don't work thata way!" and he leveled his .350 magnum and fired a round into the unsuspecting man's head almost vaporizing it, and blood and brain matter sprayed the walls of the cave and covered Rance. He spit and wiped the blood from his face with the sleeve of his coat, checked his pistol, and replaced the spent round, cocked the hammer back, and walked out into the open, firing 1...2...3...4 rounds wildly, knowing full well that he wasn't getting out of his mess alive or unharmed.

Jasper and Terry both had their sights painted on his chest when he came into view, and after the fourth shot, they both squeezed their triggers almost simultaneously, each hitting Rance in the chest just inches apart.

The smelly, blood-covered poacher was blasted off his feet, and he flew backward until most of his torso was back in the cave; his big .357 revolver lay smoking in the snow.

Jasper signaled for Terry to stay put, and he moved forward to check out the crime scene. The interior of the cave reeked from putrid flesh and wolf skins, and he found exactly what he expected: the other poacher with the majority of his head blown away and fresh blood everywhere inside the small area.

Terry and Jasper gathered the weapons and identification from the two dead men and moved Rance's body back inside, and Jasper made the call for the cleanup crew to come up the mountain and do their job.

They started back down the trail just shortly after 9 a.m. The sun was up, but the temperature was still hovering around freezing, and there was a strong wind blowing, making it seem 20 or more degrees colder.

Terry thought to herself, "If it's 32 degrees, but it feels like its 12, then why the hell isn't it 12? Anyway, it's damn cold! That's all I know!"

They rode about a quarter of a mile down the mountain, and Terry began to hear the howling of the pup once more. She pulled Biscuit up and dismounted and headed back into the brush towards the crying sounds.

The sound got louder after she had gone about 15 or 20 yards. When she reached the source of the sound, she found leaning up against a dead log was a very young black wolf with its snout in the air howling as only an abandoned wolf could. She approached the baby slowly; it couldn't have weighed more than three or four pounds, and it was shivering with tears running down its eyes. She moved even closer, and the freezing, cold animal did not seem to fear her. She figured maybe it was the weather or the fact that it was so lonely. Terry kneeled down beside it and stroked its head, and the pup turned and licked her hand several times before it went back to howling. She picked it up and held it to her chest, and it seemed to nestled down in her arms and calm itself.

She put the pup inside her heavy coat and zipped it up and headed back to Biscuit and Jasper.

When Terry came into view with a lump in her coat, Jasper warned, "It's probably not a good idea to be toting a black wolf around with ya; they don't make very good pets."

"Well maybe not, but this little guy has had a rough enough life so far; he'll die out here without his momma and her milk, and you know her hide is in that cave back there."

Just about the time they pulled into camp, Terry's phone rang, "Miss Terry, this is Abbott; how's it goin?"

"Well, alright, I guess, just cleaned up a hell of a mess over here in Glacier Park," and about that time, the pup chose to tell the world that he was really hungry, and he started howling into the mouthpiece of Terry's satellite phone.

"Whatcha got there gal? Sounds like a hand full!"

"Yes, sir. It's a young wolf pup; the poachers got his momma, and he's lookin for some groceries."

"I don't know if it's a good idea to get attached to a wolf; they don't tame too well."

"Yes, sir. I'm aware of that. I figured I'd release him back into the wild as soon as he's old enough to care for himself."

"Ok...well you be careful, ya hear?"

"Yes, sir; thank you."

"Oh, by the way, good work today."

"Thank you, sir, but I was just following Jasper's lead."

"I know, but nonetheless, good job!" and the line went dead.

Mashti means "sweet person" in Cherokee, and the wolf pup truly was, at least towards Terry.

Inside the small cabin, Terry found some powdered milk and mixed it up with warm water; then she put it into a rubber glove and poked a small hole in one finger, and her new baby went right to work like he hadn't eaten in well...forever.

"You need some time? Or are you 'bout ready to head down the mountain?" Jasper asked.

"I'll be ready in a couple of minutes."

"I'll get the pack horses ready and meet ya outside."

"Okie dokie!"

Chapter 10

The weeks flew by, and Mashti grew like a weed. The combination of Gerber's high protein baby cereal and goat's milk worked their magic, and at three months of age, he looked like a full-grown male; in fact, he may have been 30 or 40 pounds heavier than the average wolf at that age, and he never once left Terry's side. She began to realize that turning him back into the wild could present a real problem for both of them.

Up to that point, the pup had ridden in her lap in her rig everywhere they went, but soon he had taken his place in the passenger's seat, and he was even too large to sit on the console, but he always had one paw resting close, so she could stroke it as they traveled.

Terry had tried to let Mashti go back to the wild several times, but each time, he would just sit at her feet and stare into the forest without making any attempts to walk away. After three or four tries to release him, she began to realize that he was very content exactly where he was and to tell the truth, she was glad he was as she had grown very attached to the beautiful, big, black, wolf, and their bond grew closer with each passing day.

The two companions were gaining quite a reputation in the Montana region. Everyone marveled at the beautiful Indian girl and her giant black wolf, and the Indian tribes were starting to make up stories about the two even though they were a little exaggerated. Needless to say, the two were becoming quite the celebrities everywhere they went.

One day, Terry got a call from Mr. Abbott, which she knew meant it was time to go to work.

"Terry...this is Abbott. I just got a report about a couple of bear carcasses found over around Big Lake. I need you to head that way. I'll have Jasper meet ya as soon as he checks in. See Billy Three Fingers at the lodge when you arrive."

"Yes, sir! Give me about 30 minutes to pack up, and we will be on the road.

"Great...and...oh, Teresa..."

"Yes, boss?"

"Give that big ol' wolf a hug for me, will ya?"

"Ten-four, boss! Will do!"

Terry and Mashti headed southwest on Highway 2 from the Blackfoot Reservation, a place where she had become very comfortable and preferred to be when she wasn't working a case. The Indians made her feel at home, and she knew they always had her back.

She loaded up and was on the road in less than 30 minutes. Her big Ford diesel pulled the trailer like it was without a load even though Terry kept it fully supplied at all times, and she loved being on the road with her new companion.

Highway 2 afforded an incredible drive to Flathead Lake, but it was not an area where one would want to have any kind of trouble as it was very isolated to say the least, and it was a part of Montana where the poachers preferred to work for that very reason. The highway was probably only about 75 miles as the crow flies, but the winding, two-lane road made the drive close to four hours on a good day. Terry had only been that way twice before but was really excited about seeing the beautiful country again, and Mashti joined in the celebration with a couple of howls as they went.

As close as Terry could tell from her GPS, she was about 10 or 12 miles from the lodge when she passed a turnoff that she seemed to remember Jasper saying wasn't kept up any longer, so if someone was going that direction or using it, they'd be able to tell.

She slowed down and gave the turnoff a good look as she went by and then made a U-turn at the next turn around that was marked on her GPS up about a half a mile. Mashti growled low, and Terry got the feeling that he knew something was wrong as well. She drove slowly on the dirt road, which was more like a trail with absolutely no room to pass until the next parking area, maybe a half a mile or so. If it weren't for the government's up-to-date GPS, she'd have been traveling blind.

She wasn't sure if she smelled it or saw the big cabover Winnebago first, which was about 28 or 30 feet long with most of the paint and graphics scraped off from running through the rocks and brush. She pulled off the trail as much as possible and sent Jasper a text of her location then got out with her Glock in hand and made an inspection of the motorhome.

Through the windows, she could see bear skins and wolf pelts stacked in the rear of the living area and of course, the stench was an instant giveaway. She did a complete inspection of the surrounding area; then she unloaded Biscuit and saddled the anxious horse.

Next, she made a quick inspection of her rifle and ammo and made sure she had enough food and warm clothes for a couple of days, just in case. The weather, though comfortable at the time, would drop into the low 30s when the sun went down, and it was never fun to be caught out in the mountains unprepared in bad weather as there was always the chance of a storm.

She gave Gravy some hay and grain and checked his water just in case she didn't make it back that night. Then she mounted Biscuit and settled back in the saddle. She gently touched his flanks with her heels, and the big horse jumped a little, and they were off. Mashti growled low and ran ahead of Terry and her horse as though he knew exactly what he was after, and as it turned out, he did.

About a mile or so up the trail, Mashti stopped and posed with his head pointing up the trail; a few seconds later, Terry heard a gunshot that she knew came from a large-bore rifle.

The terrain had changed drastically almost to straight up and down. There was no way a horse with a rider was going to get up the trail. She tied Biscuit to a pine with plenty of green grass around, and she and the big wolf started their climb. The going was much harder for her than for Mashti, and he stayed about 15 or 20 yards ahead of her but always kept her in sight or ear shot.

Terry wasn't sure how long they'd been hiking, but she was getting winded, and she sent Mashti off to the side to inspect the situation. She finally came to a very large outcropping of boulders, and she made her way to the top to get a better feel for the terrain and where the un-subs (unknown subjects) might be.

She had just made it to the top and kneeled down when something hit her hard in the chest, and she fell backwards and rolled down the large rocks, wedging her body between two at the bottom. She was unconscious and wedged tight with a bullet hole in her left shoulder that had gone clean through without hitting any bone or damaging any muscle, fortunately for her.

Mashti was moving up the mountain working his way around rocks and tall trees, all the while knowing where the men he was looking for were located. He moved on past them a 100 yards or so then started back down the mountain and stopped on an outcropping of rocks about 15 or 20 feet above the three poachers.

The smell of blood from his master's wound was strong in his nose, but first, he had a task to perform. The sun was almost down, and the Montana moon showed red in his eyes; he dove without making a sound and landed on two of the three killers, his teeth ripping and tearing and slashing, and men were screaming in pain, and blood was spraying in all directions.

The third man was in panic mode and not used to confronting animals up close. He pulled his .357 revolver from his holster, but he had his finger in the trigger guard and squeezed before he was ready, sending a giant slug into his right knee and then down through his right foot. He let out a cry of excruciating pain, and then the black wolf hit him in the chest with all four paws, and his teeth closed around the man's throat and ripped with a force that would be hard to imagine; he bled out within seconds from his mortal wound.

Mashti stood on a rock in the light of the black Montana moon for just a moment then headed down the mountain towards Terry at full speed. He followed the scent of warm blood and came to the place where Terry was wedged. He could see her; he could get his nose close to her feet, but he had no way of getting her free when her phone rang, and Mashti knew someone was close.

He took a quick look around to mark the place then headed down the mountain as fast as his powerful body would carry him. He passed Biscuit and growled as he continued down the trail at breakneck speed. When he came to the campsite, he found that Jasper was just getting ready to mount his horse and head up the mountain. Mashti slid to a stop and howled; then he turned in circles three, maybe four times and then started back up the trail as fast as he could run with Jasper forcing his horse to try and keep up.

When they reached the spot where Biscuit was tied, Mashti jumped up and grabbed the rope on Jasper's saddle and pulled on it until Jasper put two and two together and brought the rope and a first aid kit with him up the mountain.

By the time they reached Terry, she had regained consciousness and was able to talk to them. Jasper was able to get close enough to get a rope over her head and under her arms, and Mashti was running back and forth the entire time, giving directions. As large a man as Jasper was, trying to pull 125 or 130 pounds of dead weight was almost impossible until Mashti showed up behind him and began to pull with all his strength, and Terry began to work her way slowly up the side of the crevice.

After they got Terry free, Jasper carried her down the mountain over his shoulder, and a helicopter was waiting to take her to the hospital when they arrived back where their rigs were parked because Jasper had used his satellite phone to call for one just in case before he followed Mashti up the mountain, which was good thinking on his part.

The chopper pilot wasn't too keen on taking a wolf in his chopper until he realized he didn't have much choice; the wolf was coming, or he wasn't taking off, period!

Jasper waited in the area until someone showed up to drive Terry's rig back to Helena and of course, she thought she was ready to go back to work the next day, not! The hospital staff were scared to death having to work around a very big, black, male wolf sleeping on the foot of her bed, but they managed to get Terry stitched up and sedated in spite of Mashti's massive presence.

Abbott thought he would need to remove the big animal until Jasper told him the story of the poachers and how Mashti handled the situation and all of a sudden, he was a welcomed guest with full honors.

That night, Jasper brought in two Porterhouse steaks about two inches thick, baked potatoes with the trimmings, Caesar salad, bread pudding with cranberries and rum sauce, and a bottle of Crown Royal Reserve that he snuck in in his duffle, and of course, Mashti got a full complement and only got down from Terry's bed long enough to hide his bone in the bottom of the clothes closet.

Terry was stiff as a board when the sedation wore off, and she sported black and blue bruises from head to toe along with a bump or two on her head. They checked her for a concussion, but she had none. She couldn't remember ever being that beat up, and she truly hoped that was not going to be a regular occurrence because it could get old very fast. Unfortunately, she still had several days of feeling like hammered horse crap before she started feeling better, and she knew it.

It wasn't until the fourth day that she actually began to think about getting back to her horses and trailer and inhaling some fresh Montana air. Mashti would not leave her side for anyone except Jasper and then only to make a quick potty stop on the green grass at the rear of the hospital and then straight back to Terry's room. It was to the point now that Jasper pitied anyone who tried to separate Terry and her wolf. The bond was set, and nothing could break it short of death. Three full weeks later, Terry and Mashti along with Biscuit and Gravy were headed north and east out of Helena on Highway 15, and everyone was excited to be on the road again. Terry had orders to meet up with Jasper and join the operation that was just about to close down the biggest trapping and poaching enterprise in the country belonging to Horace French.

Chapter 11

Horace French ran a funeral home in Missoula. He was a small man with little or no body hair and wore thick glasses, and he always wore a white shirt and tie and a navy-blue pinstripe suit that was out of date but pressed to perfection. He owned five suits and all of them were exactly the same. His brown wingtip shoes were always spit-polished to a tee; he just had the one pair, and the only thing that could be considered out of character for an undertaker was that Horace always carried a Glock 26, .9mm, semi-automatic pistol in the small of his back. Always!

Horace began working at the funeral parlor in 1987 at the age of 17; he had been only a junior in high school. He never associated with people his own age, and he felt much more comfortable talking to the dead, so he began showing up early and staying late for no particular reason other than he just really liked his job.

One evening while he was all alone on the property, he thought he saw one of the corpses move, and it kind of spooked him, and that's when he started carrying one of his father's guns with him to work.

Horace's job was to do the cosmetics for the recently deceased. Some just needed a little makeup or a shave and a hairdo, while others needed reconstruction from major injuries that resulted from car crashes and such.

A few months later, for no particular reason, while he was doing some repair work on the chest of a body before he dressed it, he walked away several steps, pulled his revolver, turned and fired all six shots from the old .38 caliber Police Special into the chest of the corpse. The rush he got from doing that was amazing and gave him a form of control that he had never felt in his life.

He dressed the body and put it back into a lying position in the casket to be buried without anyone ever knowing that the chest was all shot up. That was the day that his "habit" started, and no one ever caught on to what he was doing late at night.

Twenty years later in 2007 when the old man who owned the funeral home had passed on, Horace put a dozen .38 rounds in his chest before sending him to the crematorium. Afterward, though, he felt some remorse when he realized that the old man had left the business to his number one employee who was none other than Horace French.

Horace had been supplementing his income buying and selling wild animal pelts and skins for several years and was thinking of getting out of the mortuary business when the whole thing fell in his lap after the death of the original owner. The business turned out to be a great front, and Horace still got to shoot as many folks as he wanted three or four times a week when the mood struck; it was a win-win.

Terry and her brood met up with Jasper. Besides his two horses, Jasper had acquired a young blue heeler pup maybe a year or so old that someone had dumped along the highway. Jasper completely checked him out and couldn't find a single thing wrong with him that might have made his previous owner want to dump him.

"What in the hell is wrong with people?" Jasper thought to himself when he found his new companion, that he named Flash, and the two became constant companions like Terry and Mashti.

Missoula has a population of around 70,000 in the city and close to 110,000 in the county, and the University of Montana draws young folks from all over the country because of its famous recreational lifestyle and amazing landscape.

Horace French had a mountain cabin, which was more like a mansion on over 10 acres of pristine land about eight miles northeast of town that he had been building for the past 10 years, adding warehouses, workshops, and garages to process, store, and ship hides and furs.

Jerry Abbott and his crew had Horace and his operation under surveillance for quite some time but since he shipped all over the world, they wanted to make sure there was no mistake when they dropped the hammer.

Bert Cross was one of Horace French's few friends and confidants, so he did many things and got paid very well. On one particular morning, Bert was driving a large 18-wheeler headed for the lodge to meet up with Horace to haul a large load of furs to be shipped from California to China and from there to parts unknown. Bert always carried a Colt .45 semi-automatic pistol in a holster in the small of his back and a large folding knife clipped to the inside of his back pocket; he never left home without them. As a matter of fact, he never left home. He lived out of the sleeper in the back of the truck cab where he had acquired stacks of cash, McDonald's boxes and wrappers, and plastic Coke bottles. However, twinkies were his poison of choice, except for the rare occasions when he stopped to sleep in a motel and drink his fill of beer with Tequila chasers and then sweep out the trash from the sleeper once a week or so.

Bert only had two numbers saved in his cell phone: one contact was Horace, and the other was a lady he met one night in a bar down around San Diego a year or so back. However, much to Bert's disappointment, after that night whenever Bert called, she never answered her phone, so he finally quit calling her. He thought about deleting her information but didn't know how to go about it.

Bert's cell phone rang, which brought him back to reality. He looked down and frowned at the number that came up.

"Hey, boss, what's up? I'm still a couple of hours out!"

"Ok, well, the boys are here ready to load ya up; shouldn't take more than 35-40 minutes to turn ya around."

"Yes, sir! I'll back her straight into the stall when I get there; see ya soon."

Terry, Jasper, and the FEDs had managed to put a wiretap on Horace's phone, so it looked like they were finally going to put a stop to his operation. They met on a piece of property that was owned by the state that was around five acres back off the highway a quarter of a mile or so with lots of cover.

Dusty Rodes, Jasper, and Terry all met up the evening before and made camp while they planned their attack with Mashti and Flash huddled close to their masters' sides.

"It's about four miles, but with the horses, we can cut across the mountain and come in from behind, not more than a mile or so."

Jasper filled the other two in on his plan to finally shut Horace's operation down once and for all, and the FEDs left to find a spot out of sight and wait for Jasper's call to charge. Dusty, Jasper, and Terry mounted up and headed across the country to take up their positions at the back of Horace's property and wait for Bert Cross to pull his 18-wheeler into the warehouse.

Terry couldn't help but be overwhelmed by the beautiful scenery. Even though she had been in

Montana for over four months, she never tired of the amazing vistas. The three rode at a steady pace not pushing the horses too hard; they were aware of Bert Cross' location and knew they still had over an hour before he would be on the property.

When they were within half a mile of Horace's cabin, they moved down the mountain and worked their way up a canyon that skirted his property; the large rocks and trees would keep them out of his view. They tied the horses to a tree about 40 yards from where they planned to start their attack and went the rest of the way on foot.

Forty-five minutes later, right on schedule, good ol' Bert came busting through the front gate, layin on the air horn to let everyone in four counties know that he was in town, and Jasper fired up his satellite phone and instructed the other two truckloads of FEDs to start slowly moving in to close the net around the property.

The only thing that Jasper and Terry weren't exactly sure of was the number of folks who were hanging out in the warehouse and what part they would play in the battle when the shooting started.

"Hey, you fellas get off yer butts and get crackin! Let's get this truck loaded and out of here!" Horace instructed.

Two guys headed for the big roll-up door, and two more fired up their forklifts; the remaining four stood by to manhandle the pallets loaded with furs into position inside the big trailer.

Terry was at one end of the skirmish line, and Jasper was at the other, and Dusty and one of the other FEDs was standing beside a large boulder in the middle, and no one saw the RPG coming. It hit the large rock just a couple of feet from the FED standing beside it. The impact lifted the FED by Dusty off his feet and tore his flesh from his torso and did irreparable damage to his head and neck, and he was dead before his body hit the ground 10 feet behind the spot where the round exploded.

Terry pulled her rifle to her shoulder and just caught a glimpse of the rocket launcher as the shooter ducked back behind the corner of the warehouse; she put the cross hairs of her scope in that exact spot and waited a long 30 seconds until the shooter exposed himself once more. Terry squeezed the trigger, and the supersonic round buried itself in the rocket man's chest, and he flew backwards, pulling hard on the trigger as he went. The RPG was pointed directly at the big house when it went off, and a second or so later, it had traveled the 50 yards and crashed through the sliding glass doors at the rear of the big log cabin and exploded in the kitchen, starting a chain reaction from the propane lines to the stove and other appliances in that part of the big, beautiful, home, and in a matter of seconds, the entire lower level of the structure was engulfed in flames.

Bert Cross was sitting in the cab of his truck with his eyes closed listening to a Johnny Cash CD and sucking on a two-liter bottle of Coke when all hell broke loose. At the first sounds of gunfire, his reflexes squeezed the bottle, and the sugary liquid shot out all over his face and down his chest and soaked his semi-white T-shirt that he'd been wearing for the last four days, "Hey! What the hell?"

He tossed the bottle to the floorboard, opened the door, and stepped down to face the idiot who had the audacity to invade his space. As he stepped to the ground and slammed the truck door, Horace's beautiful cabin exploded, and the concussion knocked him backwards a full step. His mind wasn't fully functioning as he spun in a couple of circles trying to comprehend what had just happened. It finally dawned on him that they were being attacked, and he pulled his .45 from his belt and began firing at no one in particular.

Jasper pulled out his satellite phone and instructed the other two vehicles full of FEDs who were standing by at the front of the property to proceed with caution; then he put the cross hairs of his rife in the middle of the grungy-looking guy who was turning in circles and firing in all directions, trying to talk on his phone.

"Horace! Horace! Answer yer damn phone, will ya?" Bert yelled. His cell rang while he slid another magazine in his pistol.

"What the hell do you want?" came Horace's voice in Bert's ear.

"Who the hell are these people, and why are they blowin everthin up?"

"What people? Are you lame in the head? What the hell do you think we been doin for the last 10 years, delivering ice cream?"

"Well, what are we gonna do now, Horace?"

"I don't know about you, but I'm gettin the hell out of here!" and the line went dead.

"Horace! Horace! Don't you leave me here to take care of this mess! Horace!" he yelled into the silent phone.

Bert took one more turn and stepped directly into Jasper's sight pattern, and when he did, Jasper squeezed off a round that hit Bert in the left side of the head between his eye and ear, and his gun went flying, and he took one giant step backwards and collapsed against the big aluminum gas tank and then slid to the ground where he bled out. "Bye, bye, Bertie!"

Horace was sitting on the quad (ATV) in the carport on the far side of the mansion, trying desperately to get the engine fired up, but in all the excitement and panic, he had flooded the motor, and white smoke was all that was coming from the muffler.

"Son of a bitch, come on! Come on!" and all of a sudden, the engine caught and fired up, and Horace revved it several times to make sure he could depend on it.

All the warehouse workers had been promised a $1000 bonus if they kept the folks who were coming to steal Horace's furs from succeeding, so they all picked up arms and went to war, which was not a wise idea.

Horace turned the ATV around and headed towards the front of the house when he saw the two black SUVs turn onto his driveway a quarter mile or so away; he made a hard-left turn and headed across his front lawn and then headed south for open country.

Terry was surveying the situation when she caught Horace and his ATV out of the corner of her eye. She tried to pick him up in her sights, but the terrain kept the quad bouncing all over the place, and Horace was holding on for dear life. She checked in all directions then stood and ran towards where the horses were tied. When she reached Biscuit, she slid her rifle into the sheath, jumped aboard, and put her heels in the big horse's flanks, and they were off with Mashti running by her side.

By this time, she could see that Horace had a good half-mile head start, but she also knew that a quad was only good for about 18 miles per hour on flat ground, and it would be tough to maintain that kind of speed out there on the rocky plain. She coaxed Biscuit on and bent down low over the powerful horse's shoulders and let it pick its own way; Biscuit seemed to know what she wanted and where they were headed, and Mashti was not far to the side.

They rode hard around rocks and brush and over fallen logs, and the bouncing ATV seemed to be getting larger in her vision.

Back at the warehouse, the FEDs and Jasper had what was left of the warehouse guys in a crossfire, and they were falling like flies. After some time, the remaining three, seeing their beer drinking buddies dead, threw up their hands and surrendered.

Terry had Biscuit at a dead run, and she figured they were about a 100 yards behind Horace. The big horse was picking its way through the rough terrain and going over obstacles that would otherwise slow the quad down.

Horace was cussing and riding the ATV like a wild bronco, holding on for dear life then slamming on the brakes to maneuver around large rocks. It was better than walking but not much at times. Horace had a feeling that someone was on his tail, and he turned to see a horse and rider coming fast, which caused even more panic in the frightened man, so much so, that he began to lose what little control he had of the powerful quad.

Terry, Biscuit, and Mashti all had a feeling of success as they flew over the rough ground, closing on the out of control Horace. Terry looked again and saw the ATV clip a large rock with its front right wheel, which sent the machine hard to the left, and Horace went flying through the air, landing in a large grassy area that probably saved his life. He hit the ground knocking the breath from his lungs, and it took several seconds before he could regain his composure. By the time he was able to get to his feet, Terry, her horse, and the great wolf were a mere 30 or 40 yards out and closing fast. Horace managed to pick himself up and run eight or ten yards to a large boulder and take cover.

Terry saw Horace as he was thrown from the ATV and kept Biscuit moving forward but at a defensive angle; when she saw Horace trying run to the large rock, she reined her horse to the right to keep them out of his line of sight.

Horace checked the magazine in his Glock 26 to make sure it was full; then he pulled the slide and sent a round into the chamber and prepared for battle. Although he had never fired a gun at a live person, he knew he didn't want to die out there on the Montana plains, so his only option was to fight.

Terry was 25 yards from the boulder that Horace was using for cover, and she felt the air from the first bullet pass by her head. She sent Mashti in the other direction then kicked Biscuit in the sides and edged him on around the boulder that Horace was behind, staying just out of range for an amateur like Horace trying to hit a moving target.

As she rode hard around the big rock, her man was backing up, trying not to expose himself, which actually was keeping him completely off guard. She had her Glock 26 in her hand when she pulled Biscuit to a stop and fired a round that hit the rock just above Horace's head, and some small chunks of aggregate found Horace's right eye and blinded him temporarily; she kicked her mount in the flanks, and they were off again staying at a safe distance, keeping Horace moving backwards around the boulder.

About a quarter of the way around the big rock, Terry pulled her horse to a stop and fired again, hitting the rock about chest high a few inches in front of where he was standing, and the frightened Horace began to go back into panic mode. With all the shooting he had done over the years, he had never actually been shot at before. It was unnerving to say the least, and he did not care for it at all. He kept moving backwards and hugging the big boulder as the beautiful girl on horseback kept shooting at him, which caused him to wonder what the hell was going on?

Terry was close enough to see the fear and panic in Horace's eyes, and she figured he was about to give up or do something really stupid, but either way, she had the advantage over him, and she was going to ride him into the ground.

Horace fired three more times, but in his heart, he knew he had no chance of hitting her unless it was by a lucky shot and then what? The ATV was a wreck, and he wasn't a horseman; how was he supposed to escape?

He fired two more times, but she was gone by the time the bullets got to where he was aiming, and he was getting very frustrated as another shot hit the rock in front of his face, and the tiny pieces stung like hell. When he wiped his face, there was blood on his hand, which didn't help his panic-stricken heart. He had never been shot or stabbed or hurt in any way in his entire life, and now here he was on the Montana plain in a gunfight with a Federal agent; he began to think about the westerns his father used to watch on TV and how the good guys would walk through a wall of bullets and come out the other side unscathed, and he began to regain some of his courage. Then he remembered that he wasn't one of the good guys, and he shrank back down and hugged the rock once more.

Terry pulled Biscuit to a halt and laid her right hand across her left forearm to steady her aim, and she squeezed off two rounds that hit the big boulder just behind Horace's head, and he whimpered as small pieces of rock hit the back of his neck. He tried to climb inside the boulder, but to no avail.

Terry called out, "Horace, are you ready to give up? This isn't going to end well for you if you don't."

He heard the female voice call his name, and it sounded like an angel talking to him, "What do you want from me? I haven't done anything wrong; why don't you leave me alone?"

"Are you crazy, Horace? You're a poacher, probably the largest one in the country!"

Tears came to Horace's eyes, "I didn't want it to come to this; it just got out of hand! I'm so sorry!" he added with a sob.

Terry stepped down from Biscuit and walked toward the distraught man with her gun at her side.

"What did you think was going to happen, Mr. French?" she asked him as she walked even closer.

Horace heard music, beautiful music, like he had never heard before. The ethereal sounds coming from the female agent's voice would not let his mind focus on the present, and all he wanted was to leave this place.

Mashti was perched on the boulder just above Horace waiting for him to make an aggressive move towards Terry as she kept moving slowly in his direction.

"Why don't you put your gun down? You know this is the end, and you don't have to die."

Horace didn't answer; his eyes rolled back in his head as he listened to the beautiful music, and he smiled. As Terry got within 10 feet of him, he raised his gun, and Mashti stepped off the boulder above him and landed on his shoulders, driving his thin, boney body face-down into the ground. Horace came up with fire in his eyes and a gun in his right hand, and Mashti grabbed his wrist in his powerful jaws and snapped it like a toothpick. The emasculated undertaker screamed and then fainted.

Chapter 12

Terry led Biscuit back to the compound with Horace tied across her saddle, his hands cuffed behind his back. When he regained consciousness and realized he was draped over a horse, he almost fainted once more. He absolutely hated animals, especially horses. He could deal with kittens but only until they matured into grown cats, which was ironic considering, he didn't mind making money off an animal.

About half way back to the compound, Jasper came riding up at full speed and slid to a stop.

"Where the hell did you run off to? You scared the hell out of me!"

"I'm fine; you do know I can take care of myself, don't you?"

He had to think his answer through carefully, "Of course I do...ah...I just didn't see you leave," he was hoping that was convincing enough.

"Yeah right!"

He leaned over and put out a hand to Terry, "Climb up here and let's wrap this mess up and get back to camp. I could use a drink."

"And a movie and a steak?" she asked.

"Sounds good to me!" Jasper answered.

That evening they let their horses graze on sweet green grass and fresh water while they sat by a campfire and enjoyed thick cut T-bone steaks and baked potatoes and large tumblers of Crown Royal Reserve on the rocks. They just didn't have time for a movie as other things just seemed to take precedence. They left the dishes, and Terry decided it was time for a shower. The hot water felt so good on her sore muscles that she was shocked when she discovered Jasper was in the tiny shower with her standing close to her backside, massaging her back and kissing her shoulder. They were both squeaky clean by the time they dried each other off, and Jasper took her up into his arms and carried her off to bed. They both found what they had been waiting for, and it was as wonderful as they expected. They both woke at sunrise, trying to clear the cobwebs from their brains and figure out if Terry was in his trailer or if Jasper was in hers.

By eight, they had the horses loaded and were rolling down the mountain, heading for one of Jasper's favorite restaurants. Ham and eggs with Hatch green chilies, and flour tortillas with lots of hot coffee seemed to be the order of the day.

Terry, Jasper, and their companions pulled into the company compound about 10 miles on the other side of Missoula about 11:00 in the morning just as a very large storm cloud cracked open and dumped many buckets full of freezing water all over them. They just barely had time to board their horses and get inside before the storm broke loose.

That evening the house mom cooked steaks in cast-iron skillets and prepared twice baked potatoes and a salad with fresh greens and fresh baked sourdough rolls and magically, a giant bottle of Crown Royal Reserve appeared from who knows where.

Everyone ate like they were starved, and the serving plates were emptied in no time. Terry, Jasper, and Dusty Rodes all slept like babies in their own beds as they were all totally exhausted.

The next morning at daylight, the skies were clear, and the three Federal agents loaded their stock and headed on down the mountain with Dusty Rodes in the lead. Jasper was in the second position, and Terry brought up the rear. The road was dry, and the conditions were perfect for a road trip.

They hadn't traveled more than seven or eight miles down the highway when for no obvious reason, Dusty's truck and trailer veered hard to the right; they had just crossed a bridge over a deep ravine with a fast- running river at the bottom; there were no guard rails on the other side of the bridge, and Dusty's rig just sort of drove off the edge and began to roll down the ravine.

Terry and Jasper were helpless; they pulled to the side and watched panic-stricken as Dusty's truck and trailer picked up speed as it bounced off the rocks and tossed and turned and finally came to rest about a 100 yards down the side of the mountain on a flat spot that was the only thing that kept the rig from ending up in the rushing river.

The truck and trailer were almost unrecognizable as they were smashed out of proportion; somehow, Dusty's saddle horse managed to get out of the crushed stock trailer and was walking around with its left fore foot and leg dangling from its shoulder and a rib protruding out its side with blood gushing from the wound. It managed to stagger around in a couple of circles, and Jasper was able to see that the horse had most of the skin peeled from his face. The poor animal was obviously blind and in horrible pain; it took a couple more steps then collapsed and died on the spot.

Jasper and Terry had no way of knowing that a shooter with a high-powered sniper's rifle was 400 yards above them and had his sights on them.

Jasper was on the satellite phone to Jerry Abbott, reporting the situation, and a few minutes later, two choppers and a couple of rescue units were on the way.

Terry walked back up the road about a quarter of a mile and put rubber cones and flares out to slow traffic, and Jasper did the same in the other direction. By the time they were back to the crash site, they could hear the choppers coming their way. Five minutes later, a small four-passenger bird was on the highway, and a large rescue Huey hovered over Dusty's wreck as a couple of men repelled on ropes down to the site.

"Dusty's gone. Looks like a bullet hit the left side of his head," came the voice over Jasper and Terry's earbuds.

"What?" Terry said as she began to scan the mountain behind them,

"Jasper! Why would anyone want to kill Dusty?"

"I don't know the answer to that; maybe it was intended for me or maybe you?"

"Why would anyone want to shoot us?"

"We've made a lot of enemies in the last few months and disrupted some very large enterprises," Jasper said.

Terry felt very uncomfortable, and a chill or two ran down her back; she went to her truck and let Mashti out of his riding place in her truck. She knelt beside the great wolf and spoke softly while she held his head between her hands and looked into his eyes.

"There's someone on the mountain who wants to hurt us. Find him! Go my brother!"

Mashti took two steps and was across the road and headed up the mountain out of sight in no time.

Mashti picked up a strange scent and charged up the steep incline like a bolt of lightning, bounding over boulders and fallen logs and moving around trees and bushes without breaking stride. The hunter up the mountain didn't realize that he had just become the hunted until it was absolutely too late.

David Brown Bear was a full-blooded Indian, and his main job was to keep track of the movements of the wolves and bears for some of the poachers in the northern Montana area; he got paid in small amounts of cash and large amounts of whiskey. He was a small man, only five feet tall in his moccasins, and he weighed 120 pounds. He preferred being alone and in the mountains, so he didn't have to compare his pitiful self against the other men on the Res although he could drink as much beer and whiskey as any man alive.

David had taken the shot and watched as the Federal officer's rig hit the berm and tumbled down the mountain towards the river. The first driver wasn't his intended target; he was just a bonus. He was more interested in the woman at the back of the threesome, and he could take her anytime he wanted. She had risen to the top of the Cartel's list of people to be removed from play because they knew she was not someone they could manipulate.

He slung the strap of his rifle over his head and leaned back against the large boulder he had been using for cover and rummaged through his backpack until his hand came across a very familiar object, which he then retrieved. He had the lid unscrewed with his thumb and forefinger before it cleared the top of his pack. David took a hard pull on the large solid silver flask, a prized gift from one of the hunters he had worked for.

David realized that his employers knew exactly how to keep the loyalty of the young Indian. He was happy to take their whiskey and pretty bobbles for the most part. The first swallow from his flask was large and tasted so good that he took two more of equal size, and he closed his eyes as the liquid burned and ran down his throat; the warm sun on his face put him in a peaceful place, and he drifted off to a land where all the streams ran fast with whiskey, and he could drink his fill anytime he pleased.

He had begun to realize that the spirits in the bottle were starting to play tricks on his memory and tear at his body, but he really didn't care. All the terrible things he had done for the White man crawled through his mind when he was awake and made him crazy. He slept for 45 minutes and then woke to a strange feeling. He kept his eyes closed but felt something warm and wet fall on his face and then another drop and another. Finally, he could not stand it, and he was about to come out of his skin. He opened his eyes and looked directly into the drooling mouth of the giant black wolf.

Mashti snarled, and as David rolled to protect himself from the slashing fangs, the huge animal sank his teeth into a bony shoulder rendering his right arm virtually useless. Then he grabbed a mouth full of David's leather jacket collar and his long black ponytail and dragged him around the boulder and started down the mountain as fast as his legs would carry him.

David Brown Bear in tow bounced off of the stumps of fallen trees and rocks and through bushes. He lost consciousness shortly after the descent began and became like a ragdoll following along beside the great wolf. It was like Mashti knew what was happening, and he was going to have his "pound of flesh," even though he wasn't exactly sure where he had heard the saying.

Mashti stopped about half way down the mountain and howled, and Terry heard it at once; she trained her binoculars up the mountain and picked up the sight of Mashti dragging a body down the steep grade.

By the time the wolf with his package had reached the highway, David was pretty much unrecognizable. All anyone could see of David was just the shape of a small person covered in blood and cuts with most of his clothes ripped away, but he was still breathing.

Terry and Jasper removed what was left of the rifle and strap and drug the blood-soaked Indian to a safe place behind their rigs, and then Terry sent Mashti back up the mountain to fetch whatever was left, and the great animal was gone in a heartbeat.

"Is he going to live?" Terry asked the paramedic.

"Maybe for a while; there really ain't much left of him; that ride down the mountain purdy much did him in."

"If he comes around, call me at once, you hear?"

"Yes, ma'am! I promise!"

"I hope there's enough of that rifle left to ID it as the weapon that killed Dusty," Terry said to herself.

The big wolf arrived back at the kill sight in record time and picked up the flask and dropped it into the shooter's pack then looked around to make sure he hadn't missed anything; he picked the big sack up in his mouth and headed back down the mountain at a slightly slower pace, knowing he should be careful not to drop anything out of the pack.

When Terry and Jasper began looking through the shooter's backpack, things began to fall into place relatively fast. They found a satellite phone; a notebook full of numbers with initials by each one; the big silver flask; a couple of boxes of bullets for a high-powered rifle; an extra pair of moccasins and a poncho to protect him from the rain and cold; and four or five pounds of jerky, probably from an unsuspecting elk.

In the side pockets was a well-worn wet stone that had obviously sharpened many blades over the years along with a 32-oz water bottle and a butane BBQ lighter.

"Wow, how the times have changed!" Jasper commented, and Terry just smiled. She knew exactly what he was referring to: the days of rubbing two sticks together were dead and gone.

On the highway, Terry and Jasper had moved to the front of their rigs to make sure traffic was being controlled when she caught movement from the corner of her eye: a small figure covered in blood stood atop the barrier between the highway and the canyon and fell forward towards the raging river below, bouncing off the sharp rocks as he fell out of control into the freezing water and out of sight.

"Ah crap!"

"What is it?" Jasper asked.

"I think our shooter just went for a final swim!"

They both moved toward the barrier and saw smeared blood on the rails that David Brown Bear had stood on and then on the rocks his body had crashed against on the way down.

"Well...I guess there's no need to stick around here any longer; the cleanup crew will pick up the body down river eventually."

"We'll spend the night in Great Falls and make our way up to Malta tomorrow."

Malta, as Terry discovered, was a small town in the north-central part of Montana. The town is noted for the discovery of dinosaur remains and miles and miles of range land. There are two rivers that run close to town, and a two-lane highway that runs straight to the Canadian border, which is perfect for running furs and pelts out of the country and out into the real world from a small private airport about 20 miles north of the U.S. border, which made sense to Terry as to why they were being sent there next.

Chapter 13

Gray Marx was a very imposing man until a person got to know him. As it turned out, he was just another bully with a gang of thieves and roughnecks who weren't above putting a bullet in someone for no good reason if that person got in their face.

"Get this damn pallet loaded and get on the road, so you can get back here for another load! I feel a storm comin, and we need to get this stuff across the border!" Gray told one of his hands.

"You got it, boss!"

"Don't sass me!" Gary snapped. "Ya remind me of a manure salesman with a mouth full of samples!" one of Gary's favorite sayings, and the two truck drivers just stood there wondering what the hell they had done.

Little did Gary know that the storm he felt coming was none other than the FEDs in the form of Teresa

Littrel and Jasper Green, and they were bringing hell with them.

"Hey, damn it! If that truck is loaded, get on the road and stop sittin here like a bump-ass dog with an itchy butt on a log!" another one of his favorite sayings.

"Yes, sir, boss! On our way! We'll call ya as soon as the plane is in the air," and they climbed aboard the large-paneled truck and gunned the engine, wanting to get as far away from the big man as possible.

Terry, Mashti, and her two horses fell in behind Jasper's rig as they headed for Malta as the sun was coming up. Terry put on a pair of extra-dark sunglasses as the bright golden orb showed through the perfectly clear sky and dead into her eyes.

"Hey, Jasper! Ya got another one of them 'best places to eat in the state' in mind? My belt buckle is starting to rub against my back pocket."

"Well, ladybug, if you hadn't kept me up most of the night doin them nasty thangs, we coulda got a bite to eat earlier!"

"Hey! I'm not complaining, just sayin I could use a little fuel."

"I gotcha girl; about five miles up the road is the best breakfast in the state."

"Of course there is! Why didn't I know that?" and they both laughed, and the line went dead.

Dennis Hoffman was a tall, blonde, good-looking man in his mid-30s; one could say he looked like one of those surfer types from southern California. He had had enough of the hippies and the "dippies" and after college, he accepted the encouragement of a Federal recruiter and had been in Montana for the last seven years doing exactly what he should, and he was a good friend of Jasper's.

Dennis was working on his third cup of joe when Terry and Jasper walked in to the diner and joined him and two other agents at a table for six.

After Jasper made the introductions, they ordered their meals and then got down to planning the day's activities.

"Is that a wolf sitting in the front seat of yer rig?" Dennis asked Terry.

"Yeah. He's mostly just a good friend," Terry replied.

"And very dedicated, too," Jasper said, "so keep it friendly when yer around Terry, and everything will be fine."

They finished their excellent meals and headed towards Malta with Jasper in the lead. Terry took her usual place in the middle, and Dennis Hoffman and the other two agents brought up the rear in a big black GMC SUV loaded with all kinds of weapons and ammunition. There was enough to outfit a small army, which was basically what the crew was.

The ranch or warehouse where Gary Marx stored the pelts and furs that came in from all over the state was located about five miles north of Malta on Highway 191 and back off an old dirt road in the hills.

The compound was surrounded by a heavy growth of tall trees on all sides to keep prying eyes away. But unfortunately, it also kept occupants from seeing who was spying on them as well.

Jasper had unhooked his trailer, and Terry and Mashti hopped into Jasper's truck. There were two more agents who had the property under surveillance for the last couple of days using a high-flying drone, and they had plenty of info for Terry, Jasper, and Dennis and his boys.

"There's three or four in the main house and at least six in the warehouse, and they have plenty of firepower," the new agents reported.

"Ok, here's how it's gonna go down: Dennis you and yer boys clear the house then come and give Terry and me a hand; we're gonna take the storeroom; you two fellas keep an eye on the road to make sure no one gets away. Everybody armor up! I don't want anyone taking a bullet on my watch, and keep your communications open," Jasper instructed his crew.

All the agents suited up and got back in their vehicles and waited for Jasper's orders; ten seconds later they headed out.

"Alright, ya'll, keep yer heads down, and let's watch each other's backs; radio check!"

"Bravo 2, ready. Bravo 3, ready. Bravo 4, here; Bravo 5, ready to go!"

"Ok, this is Alpha1 and Alpha 2. Let's go kick some butt!" and dirt and rocks flew from under the tires of Jasper's truck as he accelerated out from under the cover of the tall trees toward the dirt road that led to the ranch. The bumps and ruts in the field made for a very wild ride sending their adrenalin rush even higher.

Terry had her hands around an AR-15 set on "semi" to fire one round per trigger pull rather than a burst, and Jasper had the same laid across his lap. He made it to the dirt road and turned the wheel hard left, and the big truck fish-tailed and then settled down and accelerated towards the secluded cabin and warehouse about a quarter of a mile in the distance. Jasper veered to the right and slid to a halt at the corner of the big building away from any windows, while the big black SUV peeled off to the left in the direction of the cabin about fifty yards to the south.

Jasper and Terry both bailed out and headed in separate ways, and Dennis Hoffman and his two men did the same to surround and make a forced entry into the small house.

Terry and Jasper had barely taken one step away from the truck when the windshield of the big Ford exploded, and glass flew in all directions, and a few more holes appeared on the hood.

"Hey! Damn it!" Jasper yelled under his breath.

They were caught in no man's land, and they ran with all their might to reach the side of the warehouse without taking a bullet.

Jasper had a flash-bang grenade ready and when he came to the first window, he smashed the pane with the butt of his rifle and threw the grenade in as far as possible; it went off at the count of four.

Terry had the same plan and was just a few seconds behind Jasper, and her grenade went off in the back section of the warehouse, and they both made their way to the nearest door. The front was unlocked, and Jasper made his way in and veered hard to the left and found a stack of pallets for cover.

Terry wasn't quite as lucky, and she had to spray the locking mechanism with three rounds from her AR-15 before it released, and she kicked it with her right foot to make it swing completely open. She made her entry and turned hard to the right and found cover behind several stacks of bear and wolf pelts ready to be put on pallets.

Jasper got the call just as bullets ricocheted off his cover, "Alfa 1, this is Bravo 1; the residence is clear and three bad guys are down and out, over."

"Ten-four, Bravo 1. Proceed to the warehouse with caution. I'm in the front, and Alfa 2 is in the rear, not sure how many bad guys are here, but we are taking fire, over."

"Ten-four, Alfa 1; we're on our way."

Jasper heard at least four different weapons being fired: a shotgun, a pistol, and two or more rifles, and none of them were suppressed, so he knew they were from the bad guys.

"Alfa 2, come in!"

"Alfa 2, here!"

"What's your location and situation?"

Just as Terry tried to answer Jasper, a barrage of gunfire hit all around her, and her left shoulder felt like someone had set it on fire, son-of-a-bitch!

"Alpha 2, Alpha 2, are you alright?"

"Yeah! I'm fine, just need to keep my head down a little further; let's put these assholes away and go get a drink and a steak!"

"You got it, sweet pea! Be on guard, Bravo 1; his boys are coming through the front door any second."

Gary Marx was caught completely off guard, and when the bad guy on watch at the front of the building started firing, he panicked. His finger went to the trigger of his .45, semi-automatic pistol, and he emptied the eight-round magazine before he could get his nerves under control. One of the rounds went through the top of the sneaker on his right foot and out the bottom, leaving a pool of blood forming where he stood. "Damn it!"

"Shit! What's going on? You guys better step up cuz I don't want to die here!"

As big a man as he was, he really wasn't very brave, and when the shooting started, he peed himself, and that left him just that much more embarrassed and not wanting to show himself to his men.

"You guys kill those bastards!" he screamed in a voice that could only be described as young and feminine. He hunkered down behind a couple of 50-gallon drums full of cleaning solvent, and tears came to the big man's eyes; he never thought it would come to this, and he really didn't want to die there or anyplace else for the matter.

The five other armed men were spread out around the warehouse trying to find as much cover as possible as none of them were really trained in combat situations.

Gary Marx was hiding behind his drum and firing at random out into nowhere in particular; his bullets were bouncing off the walls 12 feet high across the warehouse, and his own men were as much in harm's way as the FEDs.

Terry sent Mashti off to the left, and in no time, she heard him growl. Then the bloody screams came from behind some cardboard boxes, and two men ran for their lives as the great black wolf had his way with his captive.

Jasper was just about ready to advance when a bullet hit his right thigh, and he went down on one knee cursing under his breath. He lifted his rifle up and put the scope to his right eye and scanned the warehouse trying to find a target, just as the two who had encountered Mashti sprinted from the back of the large space, and Jasper squeezed off four or five quick rounds, and they both went down. One was dead when he hit the floor, and the other ended up with a bullet in his hip, which was non-lethal at that point.

Terry had her rifle scope to her eye and was just about to pull the trigger when the two went down; she saw the wounded man bring his gun to bare, and she squeezed off a round that hit him just above his right ear and came out his left eye, and he fell forward, dead in a pile on top of his companion.

"Everyone ok?" Jasper asked through his mouth piece. "Check in!"

"Bravo 1, 2, and 3, all ok."

Gary Marx had crawled from his hiding spot behind the drums to a spot beside a workbench that had a small door to the outside for throwing trash away. He made his way out without being seen although he did leave a trail of blood from the hole in his foot.

He made it to a relatively new Ram 2500 pickup and found the keys under the floor mat. When the big diesel roared to life, he breathed a sigh of relief and pushed the brake with his right foot even though the pain was almost unbearable; he didn't like pain, and he screamed, "DAMN IT!" as he pulled the gear shifter down into drive and gunned the engine. Sand and rocks from the unpaved parking lot flew in all directions as he did a donut in the big truck, and Marx fought to straighten it out and headed toward the road away from the gun fire.

He made the clearing between the warehouse and the cabin when six rounds hit the windshield; he never saw any of them. The first one hit him in the face just below his nose and traveled up through his brain and out the back of his head, and he was dead instantly. One of the other five hit him in the chest and any one of them would have been a kill shot if not for the job the first one had done.

The big pickup veered hard to the right and ran straight for the small cabin, increasing in speed as it went; it crashed through the outside wall and into the kitchen where it exploded and in return, ignited a butane tank that blew up the rest of the small structure.

Terry had belly-crawled around to her right and had another bad guy in her sights; she planned on just wounding him, so they could question him when the explosion from the house went off, and she flinched just as she squeezed the trigger, and the bad guy's head exploded. "Well, crap! That didn't work out so well," she said to herself.

The two goofballs returning from the airport across the Canadian border were almost to the dirt road turn off to the ranch when they saw the house explode, and the driver accelerated to get to the site, not having a clue about what was taking place.

Dennis Hoffman and his two men pulled Jasper back out of harm's way and then split up and headed towards the back of the warehouse to mop up the rest of the bad guys. The last two realized they were no match for the armed, advancing agents, and threw their weapons out in the middle of the floor and raised their hands in surrender.

The two in the truck still weren't sure what was going on when the FBI guys came up from behind, but they definitely were not interested in arguing, and they raised their hands and stepped down from their truck.

After it was all said and done, Terry sat on the edge of her triage bed in the ER with her left arm in a sling talking to Jasper in the next bed over; his leg was elevated, and he was about three-quarters high on painkillers when Jerry Abbott walked in.

"Jesus! You two sure know how to make a mess of things! Every time you get together, you blow something the hell up! Do ya'll plan that, or is it just a coincidence?"

Terry started to laugh, but the pain jabbed deep into her shoulder, which made her look around the room for a nurse and more pain meds.

"Hey, boss, please don't make me laugh! I promise we'll do better in the future and try not to blow everything up too much."

"Eh...don't worry about it. Actually, you two did a great job...cleaned up most of the poaching goin on in the state. You two make a great team! I'm thinking of keeping you together if ya don't have a problem with that."

Terry looked at Jasper and smiled, and Jasper looked at Abbott with that "higher than a kite" look on his face, and Abbott said, "I guess I can take that as a yes?"

A week and a half later, Terry and Jasper had their trailers parked side by side on the west side of the lake at East Glacier Park in a secluded area on the Indian Reservation where they could have all the privacy they required.

They both received 10 days of R&R with pay for being wounded in the line of duty. They had their ice boxes full of T-bone steaks and smoked elk ribs that the Indians had dropped by and several very large bottles of Crown Royal Reserve. The weather was beautiful, and the fish were biting, and life was perfect, at least until their next assignment.

The End!

Black Wolf Moon

Duke Charles

OTHER BOOKS BY DUKE CHARLES

LUKE KASH WESTERN SERIES
People of the Horse
Spirit and the Blood
Blood and Thunder
Thunder Cloud and Spirit Walker

ROC REESE MYSTERY SERIES
Birdies and San Diego Heat
Birdies and Vegas Heat
Birdies and Texas Riviera Heat
Birdies and New Orleans Heat
Birdies and Maui Heat

OTHER BOOKS BY DUKE
Duke Charles' Shorts
Blanco River Wars
A Texas Melody